MEXICAN GHOST TALES OF THE SOUTHWEST

STORIES AND ILLUSTRATIONS BY

ALFRED AVILA

COMPILED BY KAT AVILA

Piñata Books
Houston, Texas
1994

This book is made possible through a grant from the National Endowment for the Arts (a federal agency), the Lila Wallace-Reader's Digest Fund and the Andrew W. Mellon Foundation.

Piñata Books
A Division of Arte Público Press
University of Houston
Houston, Texas 77204-2090

Piñata Books are full of surprises!

Cover design by Daniel Lechón

Avila, Alfred
    Mexican ghost tales of the Southwest / by Alfred Avila : compiled by Kat Avila.
        p.   cm.
    ISBN 1-55885-107-0 : $9.95
        1. Mexican Americans—Folklore. 2. Tales—Southwest, New. 3. Ghost stories—Southwest, New. I. Avila, Kat. II. Title.
GR111.M49A95 1994   94-6919
398.25'0976—dc20   CIP

The paper used in this publication meets the requirements of the American National Standard for Permanence of Paper for Printed Library Materials Z39.48-1984. ∞

*To my parents, José and Guadalupe Avila,
and to Rev. John V. Coffield.
In blessed memory of Rabbi Robert J. Bergman.*

—Alfred Avila

CONTENTS

La Llorona 11

The Devil Dog.. 15

The Bad Boy.. 19

The Witches 25

The Pepper Tree.. 35

The Devil and the Match 41

The Devil Baby.. 45

The Devil's Wind 49

The Funeral and the Goat Devil 55

The Dead Man's Shoes..................................... 59

The Yaqui Indian and the Dogs..........................69

The Caves of Death.. 79

The Acorn Tree Grove 89

The Water Curse 97

The Bat... 105

The Japanese Woman 115

The Brutish Indian 129

The Whirlwind 137

The Chinese Woman of the Sea..........................145

La Llorona of the Moon 161

The Owl 169

THE STORYTELLER

MEXICAN GHOST TALES
OF THE SOUTHWEST

LA LLORONA

LA LLORONA

A long time ago, in the old days, there lived a woman in Mexico. Life was hard for her because her husband had died and she was left with three small children. In time, the children became a burden for the woman. She longed for the gaiety and the dancing at the fiestas as an escape from her daily responsibilities. For this reason, the woman would go out and leave the children to fend for themselves, and because they were hungry and hurt from the beatings they received at her hands, the children cried often.

One day, tired of hearing her children's endless weeping and pleading for food, the woman forced them into a sack and dragged them to a nearby river swollen from the rains in the mountains. Although the children cried out to their mother, begging her to release them, they did not suspect the grim fate she had in store for them.

As the woman dragged the sack slowly to the water's edge, she could hear her children cry out, "Please, mother! Please!" Still, she was determined to cast off the yoke that hung around her neck because her heart was hard and cruel.

Oh, to be rid of these troublesome children! she

thought.

Finally, the mother pushed the sack off the bank into the river with one quick move. She could hear her children's terrified screaming as they tumbled into the swift, swirling waters that swallowed them into eternity. Afterwards, the woman walked away happy. At last she was free!

The woman continued her loose wicked life until she finally died. Her soul was then taken before God for judgment. Trembling and sorrowful, she stood before the Almighty.

"You!" God said to her, "are to be pitied. Not only have you sinned greatly during your time on earth, but you committed the greatest sin of all, you killed your own children. Therefore, you are condemned to roam the rivers of the world until you find their bones. You will find no rest until then, and you will wander about crying until the end of the world."

If some night when there is no moon, you happen to hear a long, mournful, howling cry by the river, beware! It may be La Llorona, the Wailing Woman, looking for her children. Stay away from the river, because you don't want her to find you in the dark.

THE DEVIL DOG

THE DEVIL DOG

Many years ago in the quiet sleepy village of La Colonia, on the outskirts of Zacatecas, there lived a hard-drinking man who did not care for his own people. He spent the nights drinking tequila and *pulque* and quarreling at the local cantina, and the days sleeping in the dusty, windy streets.

Sometimes he made it back to his adobe house. It sat about a mile from the village, in a clump of mesquite trees amidst large cactus plants that grew here and there from the arid ground. The house was just a short distance from the railroad tracks. On rare occasions, a train would pass by headed north. It would carry federal troops sent to suppress the unrest stirred up by the famous Pancho Villa and the revolution that was blazing in the northern lands.

One night, after drinking heavily, the man said goodbye to his friends in the cantina and staggered out reeking of tequila and lime. Stumbling in the dark, he finally found his way to the railroad tracks.

"At last!" he said to himself in a drunken stupor. "I will follow the tracks home."

As he wove his way home stumbling on the railroad ties, he suddenly tripped over the rail, hitting the ties hard when he landed on the gravel.

"Oh, what a miserable life!" he cursed out loud in the dark.

As he slowly picked himself up, he looked back and saw two small red glowing lights way off in the distance. The drunkard staggered onward humming to himself, and every once in awhile he would glance backward. Each time he could see the red lights gaining on him.

The man kept walking on and thinking, "What can those lights be? Maybe they're only a pair of fireflies."

He was beginning to sober up and was perspiring. He looked back again, straining his eyes in the dark. Nearer and nearer the lights came.

He started to run, trembling from fear and gasping for breath. When he looked behind him, now mortally afraid, he saw a coal-black dog moving towards him in a fast, loping motion, a huge dog with bright glowing red eyes that gleamed in the moonless night!

The drunkard screamed and screamed, his shrieks echoing into the darkness.

Days passed, and the man was never seen again. Around the village water fountain there was gossip that he was carried off by witches, or that he got tired of the town and hopped on a train headed north to join the revolution.

"Who knows?" the villagers used to say.

What no one ever guessed was that the drunkard had been carried into Hell in the tightly clenched jaws of the Devil himself, screaming in fear for his eternal soul.

THE BAD BOY

THE BAD BOY

Many years ago somewhere in the lowlands of the Sierra Madre Mountains, there was a remote village. Life was hard for the villagers, who lived on the edge of starvation. Many managed to barely survive by selling the firewood they gathered in the surrounding hills to the people of a nearby town. With this, they earned a few coins they used to buy maize for their tortillas and a handful of beans.

On the outer edge of the village in an old adobe house lived Enrique, a sixteen-year-old boy and his mother. Enrique had worked hard collecting wood and selling it to the townspeople for their cooking from the time he was eight. By now, with no improvement to his life and every day the same grueling routine, he was getting tired of his daily chores. His mother was old and could do nothing more than sit in the house, cook the meager daily meals, and pray before the family altar. His father had died when Enrique was very young.

Every morning Enrique would rise early, grab his machete, and head for the hills to cut wood. By the end of the day, the weight of the heavy bundles bit into his shoulders, bruising them. Still, the will to survive is strong, even for the poor, and it kept Enrique going.

"Ah!" the boy would dream. "To run away to the big city of Chihuahua!"

Enrique had heard stories about the city from those friends of his who had been lucky enough to attend the large festival of the Day of the Dead held there every year. But he had never had the money for the trip. As it was, sometimes he could barely manage to feed himself and his mother, and she was beginning to get on his nerves.

"What a useless old woman!" he would say to himself. "She's like a flea on my skin! All she does is sit at home while I work hard chopping and gathering wood to sell in town in the heat of the merciless sun! Then, when I get back home, I have to go down to the village fountain to fill the water jars!"

One day he decided that he would not go out and work. His mother begged him to go do his daily chores.

"Please, son," she pleaded with him.

One day, her whining tone aggravated him more than usual. He was tired of her crying and uselessness. Enrique raised himself up and kicked at his elderly mother. Her face was suddenly covered with fear.

He yelled at her, "I'm sick of your ugly face! I'll fix you once and for all!"

He took his machete in his hands and started to hack at her. She did not even have time to scream; horror was etched on her face as he cut her down with one deadly slash. Blood flew on the wall and fell on the dirt floor as he hacked her once, twice, three, four times before his rage calmed down.

Enrique walked over to a shelf and took a small bag that held a few coins. He put them in his pocket. Then he went out of the adobe house and headed for a nearby river to wash the blood from his hands and his clothes.

"Once I clean myself up, I'll head for the city of Chihuahua," he laughed.

Upon reaching the bank of the river, he took off his clothes and washed himself. He then began to wash off the fresh blood from his garments. The trail of blood flowed in short stringy threads as it rippled and swirled away in the water. Enrique squatted on the bank with the morning sun warming his wet body.

He slowly stood up to leave. To his surprise, his feet were stuck to the sandy soil. He strained to break loose, but to no avail. He cried, and screamed for help

Some of the village people came. They pulled to break him loose, but they could not move him. He sank to his ankles. Later on during the day, they discovered the boy's ghastly deed. He had killed his mother.

In Mexico, one of the most unforgivable crimes is to kill your mother or your father, or both parents. Even the beasts in the wild do not commit such brutal acts.

As the days went by, Enrique sank deeper and deeper into the riverbank. The older women of the village took pity on him and brought him food and drink. The men made no effort to assist him. The women prayed for him.

He cried and pleaded and begged to be helped, but he only sank further into the earth. He sank to his waist, then to his chest. He could be heard at night yelling and crying for his mother to break him loose. He screamed and cried, but it helped him none. He sank to his neck. After several weeks, he disappeared into the sandy earth screaming, only screaming, until the earth swallowed him.

They marked his final resting place with an old wooden stake. Some nights, even today, he can still be heard screaming from the river's edge.

THE WITCHES

THE WITCHES

Deep in the interior of Chihuahua lies the small town of San Francisco del Oro. The Rio Conchos flows nearby, and the Sierra Madre Mountains stand on the west side. On the outskirts of the town are dry rolling hills and valleys with a few trees scattered here and there.

At the base of a nearby hill, there used to be an old adobe house guarded by a tall adobe wall. The local people would avoid going near the place once the sun started to set. They said that evil reeked from it. The tall adobe wall and the closed wooden gates kept the house separated from the outside world. No one was ever seen emerging from the place, and no one knew who lived within.

A young boy named Refugio—known as Cuco to everyone— lived in a neighboring village in a small adobe house with his father and his dog Prieto. All his life Cuco had heard stories about the haunted old house at the foot of the hill and about the horrific creatures that dwelled in it, and these discussions he overheard at the village fountain did not fail to stir his curiosity. At night, the unearthly screams he heard coming from the direction of the old house also inflamed his curiosity. Cuco and

Prieto—the dog's eyes bulging from fright—would both sit and stare in the direction of the screams.

"What is happening? Who are these creatures that rule the night?" Cuco would wonder to himself.

One night when his curiosity got the better of him, Cuco got up from his bed, slipped by his sleeping father, and left by the back door followed by Prieto who kept looking up at his master with wondering eyes. The boy and the dog crossed a field and headed down the road towards the evil adobe house, looking in all directions to make sure that they were not being followed by any of the evil creatures.

In the distance Cuco could see the silhouette of the big house and the reflection of strange flickering lights from behind the tall adobe wall that surrounded it.

When he finally reached the wall, Cuco climbed up a tree that grew next to it, going up the trunk first and then into the upper branches. Below, his dog leaped in vain trying desperately to follow. Pulling himself along one of the big branches, Cuco managed to reach the top of the wall where he was partially hidden by the tree. There he stood, panting, his heart thumping hard.

"What will my fate be if I am discovered?" he wondered. "Will evil fangs bite deep into my body and make me shrivel up?" This was a horrifying thought because Cuco could not imagine himself as a shriveled up bag of skin and bones.

As he sat quietly on the wall hidden by the tree branches, Cuco heard voices, and he looked to the roof of the old house. There he saw two women in the dark, two witches performing a terrifying ritual. They were pulling out their own eyes and replacing them with eyes plucked from live cats!

The shrieks and howls of the animals were pitiful to hear. Once they were through with the cats, the witches threw them over the wall, their bodies making a thumping noise as they hit the ground. The animals thrashed in the grass and brush in a frenzy of pain as they leaped and ran wildly, howling and screeching until death finally silenced them.

All this time Prieto, huddled under the tree next to the adobe wall, was shivering and shuddering from fright, wondering where those screaming demons that were falling from the sky had come from. Finally, although the dog was loyal to his master, he couldn't stand it any longer. His fear made him dart in the direction of the village, leaving Cuco to meet his foolish fate.

Cuco could see the two witches on the roof. They raised their arms skyward, spread them, and uttered an incantation to the King of Evil, the Devil. Membranes sprouted from their outspread arms, forming bat wings. Both witches flew up and away into the darkness of the night.

Cuco stood on the wall and repeated the secret words he had heard. He, too, felt wings sprout. The boy leaped off the wall flapping, and headed in the direction the witches had gone. He flew and flew. In the distance, he could see them landing in the far valley.

The wind had come up and was getting stronger. He found it hard to fly. As he approached the area where he had seen the witches land, Cuco could hear an eerie howling sound. He landed nearby. A tall mound hid him from the coven of witches and sorcerers. There was a curious smell in the wind. The grass was high and almost reached his shoulders.

Suddenly, he realized the cause of the howling sound. It was the wind blowing over a large deep hole in the ground that made the sound. There were many mounds and holes in the grassy area. The sound resembled the moans of the dead crying over their miserable existence in the deep pit of hell, howling to get out of their misery and knowing there is no escape. He covered his ears to block out the noise.

The grass was swirling like thousands of thin wiggling snakes as the wind came in stronger and carried the stench of death into Cuco's nostrils. It was horrible! Gasping for breath, Cuco threw himself backward into the swirling grass. The mounds were piles of decaying dead bodies!

He knew where he was now. This was the Valley of Santa Barbara, where the revolutionary forces of Pancho Villa and Emiliano Zapata had destroyed several hundred federal troops in a fierce battle. The deep holes in the grassy valley were to have been burial pits for the dead. After the battle, no one remained behind to bury the federal troops. They were hated by the peasants, so they lay in huge piles alongside the pits, unmourned, rotting food for crows and witches.

In the high grass, looking up at the mound formed by the bodies, Cuco could see the jutting arms, feet, and skulls tangled up in a giant heap. He could hear the wizards and witches feasting and haggling over the dead bodies. What a horrible feeling came over him! In the dark, the sounds and smells made him feel very sick. He sat there in the grass regretting his foolish quest.

Frightened, Cuco slowly turned and started to

walk through the tall grass away from the stench
and noise of the gathered witches and sorcerers.
He started to pray to the god of the Spaniards and
to the gods of his father, the gods of the
Tarahumara Indians. The ancient gods would protect him as they had protected his ancestors for
past generations. His bat wings vanished as he
prayed, for evil and good are not compatible.

Now Cuco could no longer fly, so he prayed as
he half ran through the tall grass, avoiding the
burial pits and the mounds of the dead. The grass
became like a thousand whips lashing at his face
and body. He ran and ran. Time became a stranger.
The world seemed to stop except for his running.
He felt an unfamiliar feeling deep within him,
egging him to keep on going. His feet kept pounding the hard ground. He lost his sandals somewhere. He was running for reasons unknown to
him, perhaps a legacy from his ancient ancestors to
run from evil, run from death, run for life . . . run.

Cuco finally made it out of the high grass and
out into the open. He was like a coyote, running
blindly ahead to escape the hunters, pushed
onward by a strong desire to live. He reached a hill
and started up the dry grassy slope. Sensing danger, he turned his head to look back. In the distant
valley, he saw two shadows rise from the earth.
The witches! They had seen him.

He started to pray in a gasping voice. "Oh, gods
of my Tarahumara fathers, help me! Help me!" he
pleaded between gasps for air.

His lungs were burning, and the wind seemed
to be pushing him back toward his deadly hunters.
He struggled forward, fighting the wind. His body
trembled. He was scared. His limbs were tight. The

air was like fire in his lungs, searing, burning.

The shadows of death, the shadows of eternal darkness, the fangs of evil were gaining on him. Cuco was beginning to tire. He was slowly losing the race for life! He scrambled up the slope, but he was too tired. He stumbled and fell to the earth.

"No use, no use!" he said to himself as he lay on the grassy slope gasping for breath. The cold wind sent shivers through his body as it chilled his perspiring limbs. He could hear the sound of distant flapping in the dark. He felt his time was coming to an end. He felt like a small rabbit caught in the bloody jaws of a coyote, struggling, knowing the end is near, but still fighting to retain its precious life.

The sound of flapping wings was getting closer. He struggled to lift himself up. He looked into the early morning sky and spotted an owl flying in the pulsing wind. The owl was a totem of his Tarahumara fathers. A sign! The gods were with him. Hope arose in his tired body. The flapping of wings was drawing closer. He looked back into the sky and saw his tormentors. They were flying high, way up in the sky. They flew knowing they had reached their prey, and they had to move fast. The dark sky was beginning to turn light. Death was but a few moments away. They would taste fresh blood, and their fangs would bite deep into his tender flesh.

Cuco sat on the grassy slope, the wind hitting his face. His final moments were near. He clasped his hands and prayed to the god of the Spaniards, repeating the prayer the village priest, Padre Juan, had taught him. Then it came, like a thousand voices of angels piercing the early morning sky, roaring and echoing across the valley. It came from a distant village—"Koo-koo-roo-koo!"—a rooster's crow calling the people of the earth to the dawn of a new day!

He looked upward and saw the witches descending, their wings shredded into a hundred pieces. They came tumbling down from the windy sky, downward, down, onto the hard surface of the arid slope. He could hear the grisly sound of bones and gristle smashing on the ground. The evil hunters were dead. The deadly plunge sent them back to the pit that had spawned them.

It is said that the crowing of the rooster has magical powers. It takes away the witch's ability to fly, robs her of her supernatural powers, and blinds her cat eyes. She becomes helpless. Woe to the witch who is caught wandering about when the rooster crows! Death becomes her reward.

Cuco lay there exhausted. He would live to walk the ancient land of his ancestors, and he would never again disobey his father and the teachings of his elders. He felt good in the gusting wind as he picked himself up and headed up the slope to his distant village.

THE PEPPER TREE

THE PEPPER TREE

The old man lived in a weather-beaten shack on the road that led to the river. He had seen many good times as well as bad times, and the fires of life had made him hard and wrinkled. His one dream was to return to his home, a small town in Chihuahua called Meoqui. But he was poor, and for this reason, he had to accept an existence of hardship and exile.

"What a life! One of these days I'll go back home," the old man would mutter to himself, dreaming of a better way.

Sometimes, sitting on a stool in front of his shack, he would look toward the grove of cottonwoods and watch the crows cackling and flying among the trees. Here and there, like lonely sentinels, grew the old pepper trees. Their ancient gnarled branches and trunks made them look like old men beseeching the clouds to release them from the curse of standing in the fields to be scorched by summer's hot sun and numbed by winter's frosty winds. The ground beneath the trees was covered with messy piles of small leaves and berries.

The wind came that night, howling and whistling around the shack. "The Devil himself," the old man mumbled as he lay down to sleep. "He's searching for evildoers to carry away."

At midnight, the clock on the wall seemed to tick louder than usual. The old man awoke suddenly and was seized with fear. Something was in the room. He peered into the darkness. A moan came softly from the other side.

"Who is it?" he asked fearfully of the moaning shadow.

"I have gold!" The voice echoed in the room. "I have gold!" it repeated again.

All the old man could do was stare across the room trembling. He wanted to say something, but fear was choking him and he could not utter a sound.

"I have gold! I have gold!" the ghost repeated again and again. Then it disappeared, and only the gentle howling of the wind could be heard.

The old man could feel the pounding of his heart. He felt faint, and his trembling hands could hardly grasp the bedding.

The next day he thought about what had occurred the night before. He told himself that he had to overcome his fear and ask the ghost about the gold and its location. "The ghost must return and reveal the secret of the gold so it can find peace in the other world," the old man reasoned. And he silently assured himself that he would succeed that night in finding out the location of the treasure.

Again that night at the hour of midnight, the ghost returned. "I have gold! I have gold!" it repeated.

The old man overcame some of his fear and in a frightened, hoarse voice asked, "Where is the gold?"

The ghost slowly answered, "In a pepper tree. In a pepper tree." And it again disappeared. The lonely hoot of an owl could be heard from the faraway pepper trees. The silence of the night returned to the shadows of the room.

"The gold escaped me again!" the old man muttered. "Perhaps tomorrow," he consoled himself as he fell into the peaceful slumber of the living.

The following night the old man was determined to learn the secret of the gold. Greed had overcome his fear. "If I find out the secret of the gold, I could return home to Meoqui and Chihuahua, to my homeland. To my country!" he exclaimed aloud. He would find out tonight.

The ticking of the clock was loud that night. He could not sleep. He could only think of the gold.

Suddenly, he heard the low moan and felt the presence of the ghost. It stood by the window, pointing in the direction of a huge pepper tree that grew beside the large grove of cottonwoods. He could not see the features of the ghost, only its tattered shroud and the bony fingers of its meatless claws pointing in the direction of that tree.

"In the pepper tree. In the pepper tree," the ghost moaned softly across the room to the now wide-eyed, greedy little old man.

As the ghost disappeared, the old man raised himself from his bed, quickly put on his serape and his leather sandals, and headed across the room. He looked out the window in the direction of the tree. "My treasure. My life!"

As he opened the door, the cold night air hit his face and a chill ran down his spine. But his mind was made up. The gold was beckoning him on. Not even the dark of the night nor its demons would stop him. The craze for gold possessed him and was the driving force that quickly moved him across the dry grassy field in the direction the ghost had pointed.

He could make out the silhouette of the pepper tree in the distance. He started to half run, looking around, hesitating at times as if he were expecting someone to step out from the darkness and wake him up from his dream.

As he approached the tree, the sky seemed to get darker and the shadows faded. The remaining light was disappearing. As he got closer to the tree, he could hear the ghostly voice softly repeat, "I have gold!" The words inflamed his desire to move onward.

Now he could make out a figure standing near the tree. "It's the ghost waiting to show me where the gold is."

As the old man got closer, he said out loud to the shrouded figure, "Where's the gold?"

The shroud slipped off the ghostly head. The old man was terrified by what he saw. A white skull gleamed in the darkness. "The Bald One, the Bald One!" he screamed in the darkness, his eyes riveted on the talking skull of Death, as the ground opened up beneath his feet.

"Your treasure is death," the ghost said as the old man plunged downward into the bottomless pit of death, his screams piercing the stillness of the night.

Don't be like the old man and let the lust for gold blind you or greed be your guide. Remember the saying that gold and greed go hand in hand, and that if you do not know when to walk away from them you could well meet their master, the Bald One, in the shade of the pepper tree.

THE DEVIL AND THE MATCH

THE DEVIL AND THE MATCH

One night, while walking down the street after drinking heavily at the local cantina, Luis felt like having a cigarette. He stopped and searched his pockets for a match, only to discover that he was out of matches. With nowhere to go for matches at that hour of the night, he happened to see a man coming down the street in the dark. He walked toward the man and asked him for a light.

The stranger did not say anything, but reached into his pocket and pulled out a small box of matches. Luis put the cigarette to his mouth and moved closer to the stranger in order to light it. As the stranger struck the match, he held the flame close to Luis' cigarette. It lit up the stranger's face. Luis tried to scream, but fright had frozen his vocal cords. He jumped back and ran down the street in haste. What he'd seen by the light of the burning match was the face of the Devil himself.

THE DEVIL BABY

THE DEVIL BABY

Two friends walked out of the cantina where they had been drinking pretty heavily. They had had their fill and were heading home to sleep it off. They felt good and happy as they walked down the street. Suddenly, the sound of a crying baby in an alley caught them by surprise. They went into the alley and started searching for the baby. The crying was coming from deep in the alley. There were no lights in the area, but they were not afraid of a crying baby. Perhaps someone had abandoned it.

They found the baby behind some broken wooden boxes and picked it up in the darkness. Both men were still a little tipsy from the tequila they had drunk earlier. They looked at the baby. It had stopped crying. It had a funny smile on its face and was making gurgling noises. The man who was holding the baby began to strain. The baby was getting heavy for him.

"What a heavy baby!" he said.

And his friend added, "What a cute baby!"

The baby looked at both of them with its wide pretty eyes and said in a very deep voice, "Yes,

what a cute baby I am!" And fangs started to grow
out of its mouth.

Startled, both men stiffened. The one holding
the baby threw it to the ground in fear, and the
men ran out of the alley and back to the cantina
much wiser and sober than before.

THE DEVIL'S WIND

THE DEVIL'S WIND

It was a warm sunny day when the pigs were slaughtered in the arid brush-filled desert within sight of the town. The flesh was cut up in small pieces and placed in large iron cauldrons used to make fried pig skins or cracklings. The hard, crackly fried skin was a delicacy among the local people. Most of the people had started early, finished their cooking, and had walked back to town to sell their wares. Only Salvador and his friend Sebastián, with his dog Pansas, were still feeding their fire and stirring their cauldron.

Once in awhile a bit of fat would boil over the lip of the cauldron. It would sizzle and pop hideously when it hit the fire. This would scare the dog, gnawing the flesh off a deep-fried bone nearby. The animal would jump up startled by the sizzling sound and move back snarling with his tail between his legs. Salvador and Sebastián would laugh at poor Pansas' fear.

Suddenly, a surge of wind arose not very far away and formed itself into a whirlwind, something quite common in dry desert areas where it is known as the Devil's Wind. The cylinder of air picked up dust, and the two men were hoping it would not move towards them for fear it would dump the swirling dust on their boiling fat and cracklings. Meanwhile, they continued stirring their pot and feeding more brush to the fire.

Strangely, the whirlwind grew in intensity, spinning in wider and wider motions and making a high-pitched howling sound. As Salvador and Sebastián—who now sensed something was wrong—watched, it grew wider and wider. Pansas, in turn, had now forgotten about his bone and stared with bulging eyes, shaking violently, hair standing on end like a frightened cat, his tail between his legs.

Pansas darted and headed toward town in a cloud of dust, and the two men heard the sound of a woman's screams churn within the howling of the wind. And as the funnel gained on them at a fast pace, the screaming face of La Llorona looked at them from the swirling wind.

"Let's go, let's go!" Salvador yelled at Sebastián while both men grabbed their pot by its hot handle and started down the road, running for their lives. In spite of their terror, however, they would not drop their hot tub of cracklings and lard, and as they fled, the pot splashed and spilled, leaving a trail of grease and pork skins on the dusty road.

Filled with terror and with the screaming whirlwind right behind them and getting closer, the two friends ran. They were beginning to tire, but their fear gave them strength. They did not look back, but they could sense La Llorona closing in on them by the feeling of doom in the air. Still they moved onward with their heavy metal pot.

Finally, they were coming close to the town. They looked back at their screaming, howling pursuer. But then, La Llorona abruptly disappeared in a swirl of dust. The two men stopped and set their pot down. It was half-empty by now because with their running much of the fat and the cracklings had spilled out. Panting and perspiring, they looked around and discovered they had actually reached the church, the first building on the out-skirts of their town.

They now understood what had happened. La Llorona could not approach the church. Because La Llorona was cursed for being evil, she was forbidden to come close to God until the end of the world. For that reason, the whirlwind vanished the moment Sebastián and Salvador reached the church. They bowed their heads and said a prayer, thanking God for saving their lives and their souls.

THE FUNERAL AND THE GOAT DEVIL

THE FUNERAL AND
THE GOAT DEVIL

The river was rising and the heavens were puffed black with rain clouds that sent a million drops of water to the earth. Small streams of water, like so many slithering snakes, flowed endlessly along the path. Above the howling wind and rain, one could hear prayers respectfully chanted by the local folk from a dilapidated shack near the riverbank. A wake was being held for an old man who had recently passed on to his ancestors.

Within the packed shack, the only free space was a narrow aisle for those who wanted to view the deceased in the open wooden casket one last time. Women huddled under their mantillas, and men clutched their sombreros tightly and shivered under wet serapes. As the sky thundered and lightning flashed, some whispered softly that this was a night for the Devil and other evil spirits.

Everyone was praying loudly when out of the darkness of the storm there appeared a woman dressed in black with a black mantilla covering her face. The hem of her soaked dress dragged along the wooden floor, and the cold air from outdoors

made everybody shiver even more. They stared at
the stranger as she walked to the front and peered
into the casket. Turning around, she gazed right
and then left at the assembled people. Moaning
softly to herself, she exited as mysteriously as she
had come.

A few moments later, a long unearthly shriek
from outside cut off the prayers of the people. The
frightened villagers strained to see what was going
on. They saw the woman in her black dress and
mantilla standing in the storm. Against the bolts of
lightning, they made out the silhouette of a goat
standing on its hind legs. They were shocked and
horrified. The accursed thing galloped away along
the now overflowing river.

The people moved quickly out of the shack and
headed up the muddy path to the hills. The swift
and churning floodwaters reached the old house
where the funeral was held, shattering it. By the
brilliant flashes of lightning, some of the villagers
could see the casket twisting downstream among
the wreckage of the house. Tears welled in their
eyes as they watched the casket with the old man
float away. There was nothing they could do. They
stood there like dead stumps on the darkened hillside. The coffin was never to be seen again.

It rained for three more days. When the sun
finally came out, the villagers no longer visited the
place by the river where the shack used to be. It was
bad luck because the Goat Devil had been there.

Today, if one listens carefully in the twilight shade
of the trees by the riverbank, one might hear the old
man croak from his mossy coffin, "I'm here! I'm here!"

"He's here! He's here!" chirp the small beeper
frogs in response.

THE DEAD MAN'S SHOES

THE DEAD MAN'S SHOES

Deep in the interior of Chihuahua, there is the quiet town of Parral, located in a small valley surrounded by soft rolling hills. In the orange glow of the evening sky, the sun was slowly sinking. It had been a long hot day for Rengo. Because he walked with a slight limp, he had been nicknamed *Rengo*, or Cripple, by the townspeople. Nobody knew his real name. He was a quiet hardworking man who traveled daily to the marketplace to sell his pottery.

His feet felt very heavy as he headed home this particular day. Because he was tired and worn out as he walked beside the town cemetery, he decided to take a shortcut through it.

A peaceful mysterious gloom permeated the area. The long shadows of the tombstones were beginning to fall across the path. They looked like guardians for the deceased standing tall and proud facing the last gleaming rays of the sun; the guardians of the graves, protecting those who had gone recently or long before.

Rengo was too tired to be bothered by his surroundings. All he could think about was getting home to a warm meal and his *pulque*, the trea-

sured liquor that quenched his thirsty soul, a
magic elixir that kept his worn-out body going.

Daydreaming, Rengo stumbled off the path and
lost his footing, falling sideways with his heavy
load. He hit the ground with a thump, sending
clouds of dust in every direction.

"Ay, Chihuahua!" he cried out as he rolled down
a small embankment. Stretched out in the dust,
waiting to regain his senses, Rengo saw that his
bundle of pottery had rolled in front of him. He
knew that some of the pottery must have broken.

"What bad luck!" he muttered while he waited
for the cloud of dust to settle.

He had raised himself up, walked over to his
bundle of pottery, and started to drag it over the
embankment when, suddenly, he spotted a pair of
dusty shoes at the foot of a grave. He let go of his
bundle and went to inspect the shoes. A smile
crossed his face.

"Almost like new," Rengo said out loud in his
happiness, swatting the shoes one against the
other to dust them off. Then he put the shoes down
and started to slap the dust from his clothes.

It was starting to get dark. He quickly picked
up the shoes and placed them inside his pottery
bundle, tied it up securely, placed it on his back,
and headed up the embankment to the path with
his limping walk.

"Oh, what luck to find a pair of shoes in such an
unusual place," he said. He was happy as he
limped along the path talking to himself.

"But I'll have to separate the broken pottery
from the good when I get home. Such bad luck to
have fallen down and dropped my pottery. There
will be less to sell tomorrow." His mind dwelled on

the material things in life, for every cent he made helped him in his daily struggle to live. His was a hand-to-mouth existence.

His stomach rumbled. "I'm hungry! I have to get home!"

Suddenly, he thought he heard a voice behind him in the distance. "Please, sir, my shoes. My feet are cold."

He turned and looked around. There was no one. He looked at the bushes and trees alongside the path, but he saw no one in the darkness. Was it a voice? Maybe it was just his rumbling stomach.

Onward he went at a quicker pace. He would hurry home to satisfy his growing hunger. As he reached the road at the edge of the cemetery, he once again thought he heard a voice. "Sir, sir! My shoes, my shoes!"

Rengo did not bother to look back. Instead, he quickly headed toward the crossroad that would take him home. "What a long, long day this has been!" he told himself as he limped down the dusty road, leaving the cemetery far behind him.

When he arrived home, Rengo set down his load of pottery on the ground and headed for the water pump. He took his hat off and pumped water into a bucket. He bent over, got some water into his cupped hands, and washed his hands, face and neck to get all the dust off.

He walked into his home and placed the shoes he had just found on the mantle. Then he went to the kitchen, got his pot of beans and his corn tortillas, and walked over to the glowing fire. He put his bean pot on it and warmed his tortillas. Soon the comforting aroma of beans and corn filled the air. He peeled a couple of garlic cloves and mashed

them with dried red peppers in his stone metate.
He then threw in a small tomatillo for good mea-
sure, ground that up in the mixture, and added a
little water to make a watery sauce. He poured the
chili mash into a small dish and set it aside. He
poured his beans into a bowl and sat down to enjoy
his meal.

"What a delicious meal!" he almost yelled. He
ripped his corn tortillas into little scoops, filled
them with beans and chili as he greedily munched,
and swallowed everything with a swig of *pulque*.

"I feel so good!" Rengo said, finishing his meal
and quietly beginning to go over the things that
had happened to him that day.

"La Llorona, the Wailing Woman, is dancing for
me tonight," Rengo observed about the dancing
shadows cast onto the adobe walls of his house by
the fire. Then, returning to his original thoughts,
he commented, "The day was not wasted after all.
Some of the pottery is broken, but I also found a
good pair of shoes I can sell."

A sound interrupted his thoughts. It sounded
like a voice somewhere outside the house. "Sir, my
shoes, please," the voice seemed to be saying.

Rengo's eyes opened wide. He stood up with a
jolt. What was that sound?

"It was probably the wind blowing outside,"
Rengo reassured himself. "I'm tired and I keep
thinking that I hear voices. It's just my tired mind
and my tired body," he told himself again.

Rengo headed for the adobe stairs that led up to
his bedroom, and as he passed by the mantle, he
grabbed the shoes.

"Tomorrow is another day," he told himself,
going slowly up the stairs.

Rengo was so tired that he had to struggle to make it up the ten steps to his bedroom upstairs. He hobbled into his room, sat on his bed, and placed the shoes on a small table next to the bed. He took off his old leather sandals and lay down, too weary to light his votive candle. He pulled the covers over his tired body wondering what type of day tomorrow would be.

Rengo was a poor Indian. His treasure was his soul rather than his material possessions. His bed was nothing but an old wooden frame with a mat and a thin mattress over it and his covers an old blanket and a serape.

As he lay in his bed listening to the wind blowing across the window, Rengo thought he heard a funny noise.

"WOOOO! My shoes . . . WOOOO! My shoes . . . WOO WOOOO!" the sound seemed to be saying.

But Rengo didn't pay much attention. He was too tired. The lids closed over his eyes and he drifted into a merciful sleep, a temporary escape from the pains and sufferings of this world.

A door creaked open downstairs, and a huge shadow came into the house and dragged itself toward the stairs. The dark figure stopped at the bottom of the stairwell, looking upward. There it stood, staring. Finally, it dragged one leg up the first step, still looking upward. Then it dragged itself up to the second step.

"Thief, where are my shoes?" the dark shadow said moaning softly.

The shadow climbed to the third step slowly, ever so slowly. All was quiet except for the snoring of the sleeping man upstairs.

It struggled up to the fourth step. Then to the

fifth.

The eyes of the huge ghostly figure were glowing red in the dark. It was mad, very mad. Rengo had stolen its shoes. There was no excuse for stealing anyone's shoes.

The monstrous figure crept up to the sixth step, moaning softly. It stopped and looked upward as if it were expecting someone to appear at the top of the steps.

"Where are my sho-o-o-es?" it moaned, dragging itself up one more step, the seventh step.

Up in the bedroom, the shoes sat on the table next to the bed. Rengo was fast asleep, the rising and lowering of his chest the only sign that he was alive.

The shadowy figure moved heavily and sluggishly on the stairs up to the eighth step. "Where are my sho-o-o-es?" it moaned.

The huge shadow made it up to the ninth step. Its red eyes glowed with hatred, and its body trembled with the struggle of making it up one more step.

At last, the ghost dragged itself up the tenth and final step, turned its head towards the bedroom door, and stared and stared as it started to creep towards Rengo's room.

"Where are my sho-o-o-es?" it moaned.

The huge shadow reached the door to Rengo's room and pushed it open. It shoved itself inside. Then it stood still by the side of the bed where Rengo slept and looked down at the old man. There it stood, staring and occasionally glancing at the shoes that sat on the table.

Asleep, Rengo was not aware of the mortal danger that stood right next to him. Outside, the wind blew across the window howling, while the cold, silvery light of the moon cast a grim shadow across the sleeping man.

Slowly, the huge figure bent over Rengo. It grabbed the sleeping man by the throat and pulled him upward with one violent motion. With Rengo dangling in midair, the ghost picked up the shoes and started back out the door.

A terrified Rengo struggled to free himself from the dead man's grip with no success. The ghost's grasping hand was like a vise that would not let go.

Rengo could hardly breathe, much less scream. He struggled and struggled as the dead man started down the stairs, dragging himself and Rengo down.

The next day when the villagers went searching for Rengo, they found a new trail that led to the cemetery. It looked as if someone had been dragged all the way to the graveyard. The trail stopped by an old grave. They never found Rengo again.

THE YAQUI INDIAN AND THE DOGS

THE YAQUI INDIAN
AND THE DOGS

This is a story of the hard lives that our fore-fathers endured. Death was their constant shadow and hunger was their curse.

The old man sat among the misty crags of the Copper Canyon in the Sierra Madre Occidental Mountains. He could see the distant valley through the morning mists. This was to be his last trip through these mountains. He had two companions with him. Both were young warriors from his tribe, a tribe of Yaquis that lived in this region.

His two companions beckoned to the old Yaqui. He picked himself up. They would start the descent here at this mountain pass. He looked around at the tall mountain peaks glistening so beautifully in the early morning sunlight. He was here with his gods among the clouds. He felt a strange, lonely feeling within himself. Soon he would descend the mountain for the last time.

Quietly, he looked behind himself and whispered, "Goodbye, my mountains, my most beloved mountains," as he followed his companions down the craggy rocks.

The sun was rising fast. His throat was parched
and he felt hunger pangs. They had been traveling
for two days. He was tiring, and only his determined effort kept him moving down the mountain.
He felt so alone, even the songs of the birds that
echoed in the canyon seemed to be calling out to
him, "Farewell and goodbye, old hunter."

Hours later, a little past high noon, they
stopped to rest again. It had been such a long time
since he had made a trip such as this. His mind
drifted back to the village in the high mountain
peaks.

Food had always been scarce. The young had to
be fed. Their survival was also the survival of the
tribe. The Yaquis had been forced to flee their rich
valleys and to run into the mountains to escape the
evil Spaniards who had enslaved some of the other
Indian tribes.

The tribe had chosen to fight and escape, rather
than be conquered and forced into Spanish slavery
and made to kneel to a foreign, bloody god. Their
will to survive kept them in the high mountains
with their Yaqui gods hovering around them. Here,
no Spanish horse or soldier could follow. But their
lives became plagued by hunger and starvation.
They could get very little food from the land.

In order for the tribe to survive, the village
elders decided by secret vote that those who had
reached their fiftieth year would be asked to leave
the village and go down into the valley to seek
their fate. This would enable the younger genera-
tion to have a larger share of the food.

Food was a critical factor, so the older genera-
tion was sacrificed for the sake of the tribe. If food
was plentiful, the old ones were allowed to remain

for another season. But as soon as hard times came, the dreaded decisions were made. Sometimes they left in groups of three and sometimes alone, to go down the mountain. Only the tribe's leaders were excluded from this rule of expulsion.

A time of famine had hit the tribe, and the old man was the only one who had reached the dreaded age of fifty. He had been chosen to leave the village the following morning. It had been hard to say goodbye to his family. His wife would be reaching the dreaded age next spring. He had hoped they might have gone down the mountain together.

But here he found himself going down the mountain with two warriors who were to accompany him three-quarters of the way. The last leg of the journey he had to make on his own. The warriors would sit and watch his descent, and any attempt on his part to return up the mountain would bring him instant death from the two warriors. These were the rules of the elders. There was to be no return, only a one-way trip for the chosen ones.

They reached the three-quarter mark, a point known as the Three Little Old Men because of the three ancient trees that stood there. Past this point, the old Yaqui would be on his own.

He looked back at his young companions, and they called out to him, "Goodbye, old one! Go with the god of the mountains!"

He called back to them, "Goodbye, my sons!"

They looked at him sadly as they watched him go down the mountain like a lonely creature lost in the vast space of the rocky landscape.

The Yaqui hiked down the mountain slowly. He would not look back, he told himself. He felt like an old wolf run out from his pack's lair. The only strong feeling within his body was survival. Survival was the key now! His limbs felt old and his body was aching, but he walked down the mountainside and into the valley. Then he headed toward the hill of huge boulders and rocks known as the Bones of Death.

Once he reached the hill, he would have to decide whether to remain there and die, or to walk further into the valley and into the village of the half-breeds and beg for his life. No Indian would ever think of going into the village. The Indians hated and feared the mestizos. Stories were told in hushed tones of the cruelties that befell any Indian who was caught in the lowland village. The lowlands had been forbidden by the elders since the great dispersion of the tribes at the hands of the Spaniards. No contact with mestizos was permitted. They were to be avoided at all costs. The rule was lifted only when the dreaded age came and the outcasts were sent down to choose their fate.

The Yaqui reached the hill of boulders and rocks. He now realized why this hill was called the Bones of Death. Everywhere lay skeletons and bits of broken bone. Large crows sat all over the rocky area. At first he felt revulsion at the sight, but he calmed down and told himself, "These are the bones of my predecessors. Why should I fear them? Why should I fear my own people?" Tears welled in his eyes. All his friends were here.

"Why? Why?" he yelled. His voice echoed down into the valley and hillsides. This frightened the crows and they all burst into flight, cawing and cawing. The noise overwhelmed the previously quiet valley.

The tired Yaqui stood in a stupor among the dark boulders with the bones at his feet lying around in a loose pattern like bird droppings on the rocks. He did not move even after the crows had settled once again among the rocks and sat there looking at him, miniature judges in their black robes ready to sentence him to death.

"What shall I do? Should I choose life and walk down to the feared mestizo village and take my chances, or should I choose death?" The old man was aware of the mass of bones scattered around him, the bones of his predecessors who had chosen death.

"All my brothers and sisters," he thought as he glanced around at the scattered bones.

He felt sad, yet within himself he felt an ancient feeling that was arising strongly, gnawing at his brain. Life, life, choose life! it said to him. He knew that this feeling would be hard to fight. You must live! his mind told him. He really wanted to live. This feeling was inbred within his soul. It was a feeling born from centuries of tribal suffering, nomadic wanderings, and battles against human adversaries and natural calamities.

He had seen so much during his lifetime. He knew that someday his wife and children would have to pass this way. The old man hoped that their journey would be merciful. The thought depressed his spirits.

The decision was his to make on this quiet lonely hillside. The sun was starting to go down and long shadows were forming across the valley floor. The light was beginning to fade. If he were to live, he needed to start down to the village now.

He looked up at the darkening sky, and at the

birds rustling their feathers and settling down to sleep. He had no food, no water, and his strength was ebbing.

"Even birds must eat, even worms must eat. Let my body feed these poor creatures after I am gone. I will stay with my brothers and sisters. My spirit will be free, and my life will not have been in vain for my death will beget life. On this earth, in order to survive we feed upon the death of one another."

His thoughts disappeared as he slowly fell asleep. The old Yaqui lay there sleeping, shivering from the cold, wrapped only in a thin deerskin.

But soon he was awake again. A cold chill ran down his back. His whole body shuddered. He heard howling and barking coming from the bottom of the darkened hillside. He could make out countless shadows leaping over the rocks and boulders in the distance. The shadows seemed to be heading up the hill toward him.

He now knew! The strong odor that he had smelled among the rocks and boulders—he remembered well now the dreaded wild dogs of the valley floor! The leaders of the tribe were aware that those who chose to starve on the hill would not suffer for long. They had known about the dogs all along!

He had no choice now. The dogs had been waiting for the darkness to set in the valley, for they only hunted at night. They sensed when a human was brought down from the mountains. If he had headed for the village of the mestizos, he might have lived! He sat there waiting, trembling.

"I want to live!" he whispered to himself as tears ran down his cheeks.

The elders had been merciful to him and the

others before him. They had given them a chance to save themselves by giving them a choice between the mestizo village and maybe life or the hill with its sure death.

He had waited too long to make his decision and had sentenced himself to death. He would be silenced forever. He could hear the dogs closing in. It would only be a matter of minutes. There was nowhere to go, to hide, or escape!

"The dogs, the hungry dogs!"

Heavy tears clouded his eyes. They were getting closer. The gods of the mountains had sealed his fate. He stood and looked up at the glittering stars in the sky. The snarling and barking of the dogs filled the air. He could hear them jumping on the rocks, over the dark boulders, on the hill known as the Bones of Death.

THE CAVES OF DEATH

THE CAVES OF DEATH

In the small towns of Chihuahua, the people speak in hushed tones of the treasures hidden in the dry hills out in the surrounding desert. They say the treasures are precious jewels, and objects of gold and silver taken by Pancho Villa during his sacking of Mexico City. They tell of the secret mule trains that moved during the night and headed north with hordes of treasure taken from the rich and the churches. In the caves that go deep into the earth, Pancho Villa buried his booty of treasure. He would take three or four men with him and travel for one or two days, find a cave, unload the mules of their heavy burdens, and hide the treasure. Then he would shove the bewildered peasant soldiers against the cave walls and execute them with a machete or shoot them with his pistols, leaving their corpses to guard the treasure forever.

Only Pancho Villa would know where the treasure was hidden. No maps were ever made. He kept the location of his booty buried in his mind. No one else would ever know where the treasure-filled caves were.

According to the Indians of the region, it is bad

luck if you try to find the Caves of Death; that it is smart to walk away if you happen to find one of these caves. They say that if you decide to go into one of them, you will first hear the voices of the dead, of the soldiers who were killed by Pancho Villa once they hid his treasure; that if you go deeper into the cave, the voices become louder and you can hear what was said when the treasure was hidden; and that if you are brave enough to keep on going, you will hear the screams of the soldiers as they were hacked or shot by Pancho Villa. As far as wandering any further than that, the Indians say to you, "Beware!" They warn that no one who has ventured that far has ever returned.

The caves are like a spider web. They let you go in like a careless fly. Then you find yourself trapped, struggling and becoming more entangled in the web. When this happens, the spider hurries over to toy with you while it weaves a shroud around you. Finally, it destroys you. And this is what happened to Polito when he accidentally wandered into the Caves of Death.

Polito, the old prospector, had endlessly searched the dry desert hills looking for gold and silver. Ever since he was a young man, he had been hoping for one rich strike. But it had always eluded him. Polito's only companions were his mule and his dog Mocos. In the villages where he occasionally stopped for supplies, the people thought of him as a crazy old man.

"Crazy old man, where is your treasure?" they would yell at him. But Polito paid them no mind. He would leave the village and return to his beloved desert and his hills.

One particular evening after returning to the

desert, Polito decided to camp out on a nearby hill because it was chilly. Just when the breeze was beginning to blow, he happened to find a cave and decided to shelter himself and his animals inside. This, he thought, would be his home for the night.

Polito unloaded his mule, started a fire, and cooked his food. After eating, the prospector fed his mule and gave Mocos the scraps left from his supper. (The dog's bony frame testified to the fact that Polito's fare was not too abundant.) Just inside the mouth of the cave, Polito's fire crackled and sent sparks of light into the darkness.

Because the wind began to blow harder, Polito moved deeper into the cave, where he lay on his humble bed. Mocos came over, stretched himself out alongside the mat, and watched the old man moving about. Finally, the dog rested his head between his paws.

The wind sounded like people whispering as it blew across the mouth of the cave, and Mocos raised his ears to better catch the sound, his head moving from side to side trying to determine the source. Polito also heard it. "Such an eerie sound," he said to himself. There was something strange about this cave, he thought.

Grabbing a burning piece of wood from the fire to use as a torch, the old prospector moved deeper into the cave to investigate. Mocos followed him.

As he advanced, the noise grew louder; the whispers became moans, the moans of people in despair, moans of suffering; sorrowful moans that made Polito tremble and his skin tingle with fear.

Still the prospector moved onward, deeper and deeper into the cave. Mocos began to whimper. The moans became voices. Suddenly, the voices stopped, and an overpowering silence was felt in the cave. Polito's torch sputtered, sending dancing shadows all over the cave walls.

"I hope the flame doesn't go out," Polito muttered. He was uneasy. He stood there in the eerie silence, listening and looking into the far reaches of the perimeter of light, and wondered what his next move should be.

The moaning suddenly started again. The moans echoed and re-echoed throughout the cave–long sad mournful moans, moans of despair. Polito stopped in his tracks after a few steps. He could feel the evil in the air. It wasn't a destructive evil; it was more like an evil that was trying to repel him, a feeling that he had entered a dimension of the supernatural, a place where he did not belong. He hesitatingly moved forward. He could not stop moving forward.

The cave was leading him downwards. He was becoming confused. He felt a spasm shoot through his old body. He stopped and raised his torch higher. There, in the flickering light of the torch, way deep in the cavern, he saw a dark shadow moving away from him. He quickened his pace in order to catch up with the shadowy figure. Moans could still be heard throughout the cave.

Mocos stopped. The dog did not want to follow, but his loyalty was stronger than his fear. He quickly moved and caught up to his master. His tail was between his legs; his hair bristled from fear.

Polito came close enough to the shadow to yell, "Hello! Who are you?" The shadowy figure stopped and stood there for awhile without turning around to answer.

Polito said again, "Hello!" but received no answer. The prospector stared at the back of the dark-robed figure. The cave had become quiet again. There was no sound. Polito stepped toward the figure, but it started moving again into the depths of the cave.

The old prospector followed. He could hear only the sounds of his leather sandals hitting the floor as he hiked further and further into the cavern. He lost track of time. He was beginning to perspire. It was becoming harder and harder to breathe. But his curiosity and fear kept him moving forward.

His dog Mocos walked alongside him in a scared, crouching manner. Fear showed in the dog's wide-open eyes. The animal's survival instinct warned him that they were moving in the direction of destruction. He sat upright, arched his back, raised his muzzle toward the roof of the cave, and let out a loud mournful howl.

"WOOOOOO! WOOOOOOOO!" he howled. The dog could not stop howling. He felt a loneliness in his breast, a deep sad loneliness.

Polito called out to him, "Quiet! Be quiet, dog!" But the howls kept coming. They were heavy-hearted, long and eerie. The dog would not stop howling.

The mysterious figure turned around suddenly and walked toward Polito. Howling filled the cave as the figure drew closer, its black robe dragging along the floor. The torch in Polito's hand quaked strongly. Mocos stopped howling then and stared in the direction of the phantom. The dog's eyes opened wider, and his trembling grew stronger. He could not move toward his beloved master.

Polito sank to his knees. His terror intensified.

The torch fell out of his hands and landed at the side of the cave where it continued to burn. Polito placed his trembling hands beside his head, grasping it in sheer fright. He sat there on the floor of the cave. His courage was completely gone. Something was wrong. This was not a treasure cave.

The moaning returned, the sad mournful suffering moans. The dark figure moved closer, raised its bony arm and pointed toward Mocos. A strong command came from the dark, draped figure, "The dog must go! It is but an animal that happened to follow you into this cavern. It does not know any better!

"Go back to the entrance!" it told the dog. Mocos understood. The dog got up and walked away toward the entrance of the cave, then stopped and looked back at his master.

"And, you, sir! It was your fate that you entered the Cave of Death and now you cannot leave!"

"Why? Why?" Polito sobbed loudly, holding his head in his hands. He was a wretched-looking figure on the cave floor.

The phantom spoke on. "You entered the Cave of Death. It is here in this cave that the souls of the dead come to await their judgment. This entrance is but one of several in the world. This cavern, deep in the entrails of the earth, is where all the departed souls gather to be judged according to their deeds in life. The angels are the witnesses, and in the Hall of Judgment, one's fate is determined— either Paradise or the Deep Pit of Evil. So you see I cannot let you go. You must be executed."

Polito screamed as Death placed its bone on Polito's shoulder. Polito sensed his physical body drop as his soul floated away. He could see the moaning souls of the dead drifting into the recesses of the cave. He saw Death standing over his lifeless body and Mocos running away. Polito let out a long mournful moan as he joined the stream of souls moving deeper into the cave.

Mocos the dog was found with Polito's mule wandering out in the desert. The Indians and mestizos from the villages wondered about Polito's disappearance. They never found him. The people fed Mocos, who would look at them with deep dark eyes. Only the dog knew what had happened to the old prospector, and he would bark and bark at the people. But he could not tell them about The Caves of Death.

THE ACORN TREE GROVE

THE ACORN TREE GROVE

The river water gleamed and flashed as the young boy waded across with his dog Sapo. The boy hesitated on a small sandbank in the middle of the river. He patted Sapo's head and rubbed it with his hand. The dog wagged his tail acknowledging his master's touch.

The boy looked at the opposite bank, at a large grove of acorn trees. "That's a good place to go into the grove," he mused. He started again to cross the river toward the acorn grove.

Once he reached the riverbank, the boy took hold of a small branch and pulled himself out of the stream onto dry land, where Sapo was already shaking the excess water off his body.

As the boy and the dog wandered into the grove, they heard a sad, mournful sound from the treetops: "Coo, coo, coo!" The sound kept repeating itself as they walked deeper and deeper into the trees. It was the call of a mourning dove.

Beneath Mundo's (that was the boy's name) and Sapo's feet there was a blanket of leaves that made a crushing sound when the boy and the dog walked on it. Near the hillside, Mundo noticed that the trees were larger and the grove was thicker in the area, so that very little sunlight could filter through the branches.

"What a gloomy, dark place," Mundo said. In the meantime, while a cricket in the shadows made a chirping sound, Sapo was sticking his nose into piles of leaves sniffing and sniffing.

After awhile Mundo realized that he had lost track of time. It was very silent in the grove with no other sound except for the sad call of the mourning dove. Standing in the shadows of the grove, Mundo began to remember the many stories of the river that the old men from the barrio told when they gathered to gossip and exchange tales. He also began to regret that he had not listened to his mother when she warned him to stay away from the Río Hondo because of the strange things that had happened there.

Now it was completely silent. The mourning dove had quit its cooing. Mundo sensed that something was wrong. There was a very strange odor in the air. Sapo's ears perked up as if listening to something. Worried, Mundo decided to turn back and find his way to the riverbank. But he could not remember how he had come. The only sound now was the crackling of the dry leaves under his feet, and around him it was getting darker and darker.

"The sun is going down. I must get back to the riverbank before it disappears," he said to himself.

Mundo did not know how long he had been in the grove, though he thought he had at least a couple of hours before sunset. He did not want to be caught by the river at night. Finally, Mundo thought he could hear the gurgling of the river and he began to make his way toward the sound. It was then that, suddenly, the boy was engulfed by a

huge shadow from behind. The loud growling of his
dog alerted him. The hair on the animal stood on
end while he arched his back and showed his fangs,
preparing to attack. Startled, Mundo turned to see
what was happening. He stared ahead with Sapo
snarling by his side. In front of them was a huge
cone of leaves, rising, swirling faster and faster,
and on the upper reaches of the swirling, growing
pile was the head of the feared one.

Mundo could not speak or scream from the terror he felt; he was covered with goose pimples. He
knew who that head belonged to. It was La
Llorona, the Wailing Woman. Everybody knew her.
It was folly to attempt to run from her. In that
moment of terror, he remembered the stories he
had heard from his mother and his elders, that
whomever is caught in La Llorona's clutches has
but one fate: Death.

"I am doomed to die this day! How foolish I've
been!" Mundo whimpered.

La Llorona looked down on the boy, smiling
viciously. A loud, terrible scream came from her
mouth as the swirling column moved forward slowly, very slowly, enjoying the terror of her two victims.

Mundo knew what was about to happen. But
although every nerve in his body screamed, "Run!
Run" to in his brain, he remained frozen, staring at
La Llorona. Her jet-black eyes stared back down at
him while her infernal screaming rang over the
whirlwind of leaves.

Sapo crouched, snarling, determined to fight for
his life, muscles flexed, blood pumping hard
through his tense body.

The swirling mass of leaves came closer and

closer, and the screams became louder. Mundo clenched his fists. Tears streamed down his cheeks as he stood in the shadowy darkness waiting for the end. His sobs became frightened spasms when he saw through his misty eyes the huge, screaming fang-filled mouth approaching and the jet-black eyes piercing through him. The end was drawing near. Sapo was barking and snarling in a last show of force.

Then, like the sound of a bugle in the height of battle, a loud sad cry of misery and suffering came from a distant acorn tree, filling the grove. "Coo, coo, coo!" It was the call of the mourning dove.

The vicious whirlwind came to a sudden stop. The huge mass of leaves drifted then tumbled to earth. La Llorona had vanished, dissolving into nothingness.

What had happened? What had driven La Llorona away?

According to the barrio elders, all the birds in Noah's ark were white. First, Noah chose a white raven to check the waters on the earth and report back to him if they had come down. But the raven did not return. It flew around and landed on the floating corpses of those who had drowned in the flood. It pecked their eyes out. In punishment, its white feathers were made black.

Next, Noah sent a white dove to check the waters. The dove, tired from flying over the waters, decided to rest on a mountain peak and wash its feet. Because it did not return on time to report to Noah, it was also punished. Its white feathers were turned gray and its feet became a bright red color. For this reason, the mourning dove cries so sadly and with such misery and shame. (Noah had to send out another dove to finish the job.)

From that time forward when the mourning dove looks down at its red feet and sees its gray feathers, the memory of the shameful punishment it suffered for its wicked mistake makes it cry. In the same manner, that evening in the acorn tree grove by the banks of the Río Hondo, the sad mourning sound of the dove made La Llorona remember her own wickedness; how she was condemned to roam the rivers of the world for killing her own children. Overpowered by her feeling of guilt, she vanished.

When it was all over, Mundo and Sapo turned and ran toward the sound of the river. They ran through the fallen leaves as if they were rabbits chased by foxes. They jumped into the stream and headed for home running, running without looking back, splashing across the river, across the sandbars, climbing the opposite bank of the river and across the fields. The low mournful cooing of a dove in the dark acorn tree grove and the sound of the churning waters of the Rio Hondo filled the night.

THE WATER CURSE

THE WATER CURSE

There was an old lady in the barrio who was the local folk healer. She was known for her cures and prophecies. She was very respected by the folk in the community.

One day, while she was walking home along the potholed dirt road, she spotted two young boys throwing stones at a fence with a knothole in one of the boards. They were missing the hole and the stones were making a popping noise as they bounced off the fence. The dog behind the fence was barking furiously at the young hoodlums.

The old lady stopped and called them over. "Hey, boys! Come here, both of you!" They stopped throwing their stones and sheepishly walked over to her in a lazy uncaring manner.

"What do you want, lady?"

The old lady stared at them with a serious expression on her face that scared them a little. They felt very uncomfortable and a slight tremor shook their bodies.

"What are your names, boys?" she asked.

"My name is Chava," one boy spoke up, "and this is Chino, my cousin."

She snapped at them. "You shouldn't be throwing

rocks at that fence and bothering the dog! I'm going to talk to your parents about this!"

Then she walked over to Chino and pointed her walking stick at him. "And you, why do you stare at me? I know you, Chinito! I remember the day you were born. You have the curse of the water on you! Stay away from the river! Your mother was cursed by the Witch of the Waters before you were born. So be careful. Avoid the river and always be on guard. You carry that curse! Beware, Chinito! Beware! You are still young and do not understand these things," she said.

Chino and Chava laughed at her. They slowly turned around and ran away laughing. They could hear her voice saying, "Bad boys!"

The boys ran down the road toward the river. Beside the road they grabbed the branches of the pepper trees, pulled on them, and released them. The branches snapped away with a fast swinging motion, crashing upward into the other branches so that leaves and berries fell on their heads. The boys ran to a place where a sandbar dammed the swirling waters of the San Gabriel River, forming a large pond. A green mantle of watercress covered the serene waters of the pond. The large cottonwood trees on the riverbank cast dark shadows over the water while killdeer birds flew over the river screeching "ti-el-deo! ti-el-deo!"

From the bank, the two boys tried to skip stones across the pond into the river, but the watercress would catch the stones. Then, the stones were swallowed by the pond.

Bored with their game, Chava suggested to Chino that they go catch crawfish in the watercress, and after rolling up their pant legs, they entered the water and eased their way slowly among the watercress. At their approach, the small minnows that swam in the shallow waters of the pond—knee-deep in most places—swam away.

Chino and Chava were having a great time. They would each capture a crawfish and wade out of the water to the top of the riverbank. There they would release them to see which one would move faster toward the water. They had fun watching and laughing as the crawfish moved, stopped, quickly crawled again toward the water's edge, and then darted into the watercress, tailfirst! The boys continued their game for some time. Then they tired and headed out of the water.

Something suddenly grabbed Chino by the leg, and the startled boy tried to shake it lose. He struggled and struggled with no success, managing only to fall into the pond.

"Help me, Chava!" Chino cried out to his cousin, so scared that he started to cry. "Something has grabbed my leg and won't let me go!"

Excited and scared, Chava leaped into the pond, and took hold of Chino's arms. But hard as Chava pulled, he could not break Chino loose from whatever was dragging him away.

"Help! Help!" Chava called out in vain for someone to come help him rescue Chino. In response, the killdeer birds filled the air with excited cries as if sensing the desperate struggle that was taking place, the daily struggle between life and death that is part of life.

Chino continued twisting and kicking with his one free leg as he tried to free himself. In the meantime, Chava kept pulling and screaming for help. But Chava was, after all, just a small boy, and he was weakening. Finally, he lost his grip and broke away from Chino.

Now Chino flailed, his arms grabbing handfuls of watercress and his screams piercing the air. The force was slowly dragging him to where the water was deeper, to the deepest part of the pond. Chava, with water up to his chest, could no longer reach out to his cousin. All he could do was stand there helplessly and watch.

Suddenly, Chino's body was jerked viciously downward. His screams were silenced as he was pulled violently into the water. The watercress and water swirled angrily over the spot where he disappeared. Bubbles of air came bursting onto the surface. Then there was only silence. The ripples died out as the last bubbles burst on the surface of the water. The watercress was broken all the way to the spot where Chino had disappeared.

Chava stood there in the watercress with tears streaming down his cheeks. His body shuddered as his sobbing came bursting out from his chest. He moved out of the water, pushing the watercress from him as he made his way to the bank. He walked up onto the riverbank, sat down sobbing, and stared through his tearful eyes at the hole in the watercress, the spot in the pond where Chino was last seen. Then he picked himself up and headed home.

Later, the men from the barrio came with torches to search the pond. They tore down the sandbank to empty the water of the pond into the river. But they could not find Chino's body. Inexplicably, no trace of the boy was ever found.

Only the old witch understood what had taken place in that watercress-covered pond by the San

Gabriel River. These ignorant people, the old woman thought. They don't realize that along with their ancestors, they are to blame for what happened to the little boy. These mestizos accepted the god of the Spaniards, she said to herself, neglecting the gods of their ancestral Indian fathers, neglecting to offer them the sacrifices they demanded and received in the old days. For centuries, the gods who had looked after the people waited in vain for a sacrifice while the sons and daughters of the old Indians burned candles and sweet incense to their new god, prayed to him in a strange tongue and sang foreign melodies.

The forgotten gods decided to exact their revenge. They sent the Mother of the Earth and the Waters—Coatlicue—the goddess from which all things were born, to demand the forgotten tribute of sacrifice from the mestizos. She came with a vengeance to grab the sacrificial victim herself.

The gods had waited centuries for a sacrifice and would not wait any longer. They would now return and start the sacrificial rituals again. Their victims chosen would be born with the water curse on their souls. The witch knew what had happened, but she would not tell the people.

Now, in the summer when the watercress is in bloom, the people from the barrio, seeing the white gleaming mantle of flowers that covers what is left of the pond, call it Chino's Shroud.

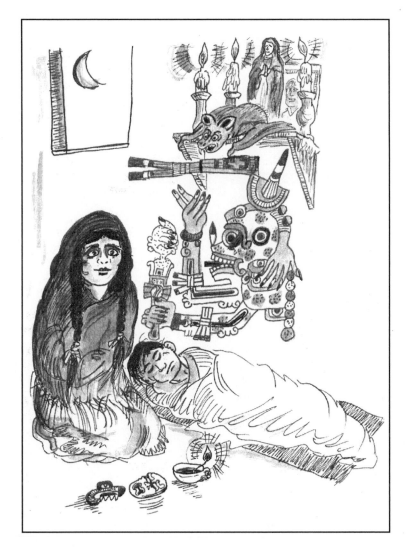

THE BAT

THE BAT

It was a ghostly vaporous image floating in the night air. Suddenly, it transformed itself into a bat and flew through the window of the adobe house. It circled the room, then landed on a small altar hanging on the wall. From the family altar, wisps of smoke rose from candles that burned slowly for foreign saints and the long-remembered ancestors of the living.

The bat looked down at a sleeping young boy, who was awakened by the high-pitched screeching of the bat. The boy sat up upon his mat and stared at the bat. He was frightened and was still trying to wake up completely. The bat cast a huge shadow over him.

The bat slowly began to speak. "I was once a great Aztec warrior who was killed in the midst of a great battle against the despised Spaniards. Many of us perished in skirmishes against that hated, greedy foe. They only sought gold and the enslavement of our people. Even some of our Indian enemies joined them. They killed our beloved priests, burned our sacred codices, and destroyed our sacred temples. Nothing was spared by this evil, degenerate foe."

"We the warriors who perished in battle are now forced to wander aimlessly in the darkness of the night. Our spirits can find no peace or rest, for there are neither temples to offer us sacrifices nor priests to ask our gods for favors. Only the sacrifice of a Spaniard or a mestizo with that cursed Spanish blood can help us. By wishing him sick until he dies, he then becomes our slave guide that will lead us to the other world.

"I have come and chosen you for my slave guide. I will come every night and watch your sickness grow until you perish. You will become my slave guide, and my spirit will finally rest with the gods for eternity."

The bat quit speaking and stood there on the shelf looking down at the boy. The child was tired and lay back on his mat, falling into a deep sleep. With twilight approaching, the bat flew out the window and disappeared.

The next day, the mother sat down by her son and found him perspiring heavily and comatose. He had a terrible fever. She wet a rag with cold water from the well and wiped his face and upper body. She was fearful and prayed to her foreign Spanish saints and gods for assistance, but none was forthcoming. Her prayers went unanswered. The boy grew sicker and weaker despite her attempts to cure him.

Finally, she decided to call María Luisa, the town's healer, or *curandera*. María Luisa would know what to do. The child was very sick and lay dying, growing weaker and weaker by the day. The *curandera* told the mother that something evil had put a curse on her son. She placed ancient Indian charms beside the boy and lit an oil lamp to keep the unknown demon from taking the child's life. A battle was beginning between light and darkness, good and evil. The healer was not aware that she was pitted against a great force, and that force was Mictlantecuhtli, the Aztec god of death, and his cohort the bat who sought release from its sufferings.

Night was arriving. The light of the burning candles sent flickering shadows against the walls of the adobe room. The young boy was lying on the mat, and the healer sat on the floor beside him. In an instant of a flickering shadow, a bat flew into the room with a high piercing shriek, landing on the small altar. It stared at the boy with black, shiny eyes, finally settling its gaze on the woman who sat quietly staring at the beast. Her Indian eyes flashed in the candlelight.

"WHO . . . ARE . . . YOU?" the bat asked the *curandera* slowly, as if forcing the words out.

"My name is María Luisa," answered the healer as she glared at the small beast, "I know that you are on an evil quest, but I, too, am on a quest to do battle with you for this child's life!"

The bat sized her up with its dark beady eyes. "You don't have the power to match wits with me, peasant woman! You shall not stop me in my sacred quest! I have the blessing of Mictlantecuhtli, the King of the Abyss. You are a foolish woman for attempting to thwart my wishes, and you will pay dearly for this interference." The animal's eyes were filled with much hatred, as it flapped its membrane wings defiantly.

"You have the power of the night," said the *curandera*, "but the day belongs to me, foolish creature! You must hide yourself from the sun, lest you become blind and burst into flames in the glow of its rays. Then you will turn into the dust of the ancient ones and lose your chance for eternal life in the abode of our old gods."

The bat knew the power of the *curandera* and could sense her commitment to the boy's soul. Said the bat, "I am the master of the dark, and you have interfered with my quest, María Luisa. I shall leave you tonight, but tomorrow I will return determined to overcome your defenses. The boy belongs to me! And his soul shall be mine! Beware, María Luisa!" The bat spread its wings and darted out the window.

The *curandera* knew that the following night would be a difficult one and a challenge, too. She sat there thinking about how to fight the bat. The bat is a small creature, but as an adversary it is a giant. Its knowledge of evil is infinite.

"The bat will be difficult to deal with. It has the blessing of Mictlantecuhtli," she said to herself. She chanted an incantation to the gods of her ancestors, the powerful Indian gods of the past. She lit incense. The sweet-smelling smoke rose with pulsating swirls and covered the small adobe room. The *curandera's* voice rose to a high pitch, beseeching the gods to help her save the young boy's body and soul from the evil powers. Slowly she sank to the floor from her standing position and watched the smoke rise from the incense-burning can on the dirt floor. Her eyes glowed strangely. She knew what she had to do.

At twilight, she was once again in the boy's room. She got a small pot and applied some sticky gum to the edges of the altar mantle. Then she waited for the dreaded little bat to arrive.

Soon after darkness had settled, a flapping of

wings and a screech were heard as the bat flew in through the window and perched on the altar.

It checked the young boy. The child lay with eyes closed, breathing laboriously. "A good sign. The boy is weakening and dying. He will soon be mine," the beast said to himself. Next, it shifted its black bulbous eyes to María Luisa, the *curandera*. It looked hard at her and said, "Well, María Luisa, it looks like your precious ward will not last much longer!"

María Luisa didn't seem to be bothered by the bat's remark.

"Mr. Bat, tell me about the wonders of your ancient Aztec empire. You have a vast knowledge of the past. I would enjoy learning from you."

The bat eyed her suspiciously, but since she seemed to be sincere, it began to tell her of the sacrificial rituals, the battles for captives, and the glory of the empire. Whenever it stopped talking, she would egg it on to tell her more. They both lost track of time. Suddenly, the small ugly bat stopped talking.

"What are you up to, old hag?" the bat said. But the healer remained silent.

The sick young boy shifted positions on the mat. In his delirium, he started to speak in a soft voice: "Bat . . . bat, why do you come here? What do you want? My soul? What do you want, little rat? What do you want from me? My soul is not yours. It isn't for you! The abyss is waiting for you. There is nothing here! Leave, evil thing. Go without me!" Then the boy returned to his deep sleep.

The bat looked down at the boy. "Bad boy! You're going to die!"

The *curandera* stared at the bat. The bat

became uneasy and said, "The morning is coming! I have to be leaving you, but the boy will die soon and become my guide into the spirit world. Then I will find eternal rest! You have lost the battle. You have lost!"

"Don't go, little mouse!" said María Luisa with a smile on her face. "You still have time."

The bat sensed something was wrong. Its instincts told it to beware. It flapped its wings nervously, but its feet would not move. The glue had hardened, and the animal could not break free and move its small clawed feet. They were stuck to the altar mantle.

"You cursed woman!" the beast shrieked, "You tricked me! You tricked me!"

"Yes," said María Luisa, "I tricked you, and you are trapped! The dawn is arriving, and you shall perish in the rays of the sunlight. You shall cause no more harm in this town."

The bat screeched and screeched, flapping furiously to free itself. But it was only succeeding in tiring itself out. It stopped and glared at the *curandera*. "My master will be very mad. You'd better release me!"

The folk healer sat on the floor relaxed, watching the struggling bat. Dawn was breaking and the darkness was slowly beginning to fade. The evil bat was nervous and struggling hard to free itself. But the glue held it fast.

The beast shrieked at the healer, "What do you want from me?!"

"I don't want anything from you, bat! I want to see your master, Mictlantecuhtli, King of the Abyss!" she said.

With those words, the earthen floor cracked

open and smoke poured out of the earth. Mictlantecuhtli, the Lord of the Dead, appeared in the
hole, but only up to his waist.

"Why do you bother my messenger of evil?
What do you want, you dried-up old chili-pepper
hag?" he said with a sneer.

María Luisa grabbed her walking stick and
struck him on the head.

"Don't hit me!" he screamed.

"Well, behave yourself," she said, "or I'll hit you
again! You must promise me that you'll never harm
this boy again or anyone else in this town!"

"All right, all right," said the evil one, "I
promise to leave this rotten town alone."

The *curandera* looked sternly at him and said,
"You have made a bargain with me. Woe to you if
you break it!" The sun was beginning to shine over
the surrounding hills and valleys. "Go now and
take your little evil bat with you!"

Mictlantecuhtli looked at the woman with her
walking stick in her hand pointed toward him. He
didn't dare risk another blow, so he quickly
grabbed the bat off the altar mantle. It let out a
loud painful screech as it was pulled off. With one
swift movement, they both sank into the hole in
the earth. Then the hole closed back up.

María Luisa became famous in the valley for
her craftiness in overcoming Mictlantecuhtli and
the bat. The boy got well, and some say that he
grew up to become the famous revolutionary
leader, Francisco Villa, better known to all as
Pancho Villa.

THE JAPANESE WOMAN

THE JAPANESE WOMAN

There is a story dating back to the days when the Spanish sailed the vast expanses of the Pacific. It is the story of a funerary urn taken by a Manila trade galleon from Japan to the Philippine Islands, and from there to the west coast of New Spain, as Mexico was known at the time.

The urn was beautiful. It was decorated with white and gold cherry blossoms, and it still held the ashes of an unknown Japanese person.

There is no record of the urn's history before it was brought to Mexico. It might have been offered to a Spanish sailor by some uncaring beggar, or maybe it was stolen from a Buddhist temple and sold as a souvenir. What is known is that the sailor took it on board the galleon, and that on his return to his home port of Acapulco, he fell short of cash and sold it to a shopkeeper. Later, the shopkeeper asked a friend of his, an old seagoing sailor, what he thought of the jar.

"It's heavy. Let's open it and check its contents," this second sailor suggested.

Anticipating some item of value, the two men opened the urn only to find ashes and bits and pieces of human bone charred by a crematory fire.

Shocked, the shopkeeper asked his friend to kindly dispose of the ashes and the urn, something the sailor agreed to do on his way home while on shore leave.

The following morning, the sailor left the area and headed down the long dusty road home to Atoyac, a small town about three days travel from Acapulco.

On the second day, as he walked in the hot blazing sun, the weight of the urn became a small burden to him and was sapping his strength. The old sailor felt sorry for the unknown person. He had wanted to bury the urn in Acapulco, but he did not have that much money. The local priest had refused to accept the urn because the deceased had been a heathen.

The sailor was getting tired of the extra weight. He stopped to rest alongside the road by a large cactus patch. He decided to leave the urn in the undergrowth where it could remain unnoticed and undisturbed. He walked into the cactus patch, entered as far as he could, and set the urn down. He wrapped it in an old serape because he felt bad about leaving the deceased in this place.

"At least he will be warm and protected against the elements," the old sailor said.

He knelt in the undergrowth, said a prayer, and apologized for having to abandon the deceased so far from a cemetery. He slowly turned and walked back toward the road. He looked back one last time, feeling very sorry for his action. It was not the nature of his people to treat the dead so uncaringly, but he had no choice. His village was still too far for him to continue carrying the heavy urn.

Walking away from the cactus patch, the sailor

felt the same desolation as when one of his ship-
mates was buried at sea and the only thing that he
could see after the body plunged down into the
waters was a bit of white foam on the surface of the
ocean. Down, down it would go into the darkness of
the deep where only the dead themselves would
know where their final resting place was, the sailor
thought sadly. In the same manner, no one would
ever know the final resting place of the poor soul
whose ashes were held in the Japanese urn.

Once more the sailor stopped briefly for a backward glance at the cactus patch. It was then that a
horrible, spine-chilling screech, like the yowling of
a large cat, pierced the air.

"It's probably a puma," he said, moving away as
fast as he could. "I'm lucky to get away with my
life! Little did I dream the cactus patch was the
home of a deadly cat, or for all I know, the Devil,"
he added with relief later, once he had put some
safe distance between himself and the source of the
terrible cry, making the sign of the cross on his
forehead, his chest, and his lips,   The man was
still muttering to himself as he headed home down
the dry, dusty road heading home.

The days passed into weeks and months. The
urn sat in the brushy undergrowth forgotten, in
the shadows of the cactus trees. But soon stories
were heard of a haunted cactus patch by the road
out in the lonely countryside. Indians and mestizos
alike would avoid the area after the evening twilight. It was not a safe place to be, they said.

A large fireball would appear at night by the
cactus patch. It would float and move in various
directions over the dirt road, and then it would
vanish. This was usually followed by a loud screech

and a howl of what sounded like a puma or some sort of large cat.

Sometimes the wailing and moaning of a woman in much emotional pain and sorrow could be heard. There was one peculiar thing though. The ghostly woman mourned in a foreign tongue and could not be understood. The words sounded like Spanish, maybe Indian, but the language was unknown to all.

A few Indians said that on moonlit nights they could see an odd-looking cat—bigger than a puma, three times larger than a puma. It would howl and screech in the faint light. It had not one, but four hairy tails waving in the air. The next day a traveler would usually be found dead and mangled on the road by the cactus patch.

Everyone in the vicinity lived in fear. At night they would not even venture to the village well for water.

"The work of the Devil," some folks whispered, as if they were afraid they might be heard. "The Devil has come in the form of a four-tailed cat to take souls to the Dark Pit. We are hopeless. We are but poor hardworking Indians and peasants. Why does he come to torment us? Have we not suffered enough in this sad life?"

They lit candles and burned incense to the ancient gods. Others prayed to the god of the Spaniards. But to no avail. The killings continued on the lonely road by the cactus patch. Woe to the ignorant traveler who passed the cactus patch at night. He became a sacrifice for the strange demon.

Some of the villagers went to see the local *curandera*, or healer. She was their last hope. She would be able to enter the spirit world, seek the reasons for the demon's terrible acts, and know how to pacify it.

That evening, the locals gathered in front of the *curandera's* hut. She came out and lit a half-circle of torches made from thick tree branches soaked in resin. She stood tall behind the burning torches. She pulled out a button of peyote, the sacred god spirit of the *curanderas* and the Tarahumara Indian shamans. With this, she would be able to enter the spirit world and be protected from the evil spirits she would meet.

The villagers watched as she stood in the flickering light, waving her arms wildly over the flames and chanting the secret words that would put her in a trance. She waved, twisted, and chanted. Suddenly, she stopped. Her eyes became white and she spoke in a a foreign tongue.

"Watakushi no haka, doko ni arimasu ka? Watakushi wa sabishii desu! . . . My grave, where is it? I am so lonely! . . ."

The *curandera* shuddered as she continued in the same language. "Where am I? This is not my land. . . . This dry, hot, and windy land is strange. It is filled with strange-looking people unknown to me and with strange smells and sounds!

"I was removed from my grave, from the temple grounds of Shinsho, near the village of Katsura. Oh, how I miss the green pine trees! I long for the bamboo groves and mountains of my province. I miss the winter snows.

"What place is this? . . . Am I in Hell? The crying ghost screamed as if it were in terrifying pain. The *curandera's* body shook violently.

The people could do nothing other than stare at the *curandera*. She was in a trance, possessed by a

demon who spoke gibberish. They could not understand a single word coming out of her mouth.

"Do you people . . . understand? Oh, dear! How
cruel, how cruel!" The Japanese words continued
pouring from the healer's lips.

Then the healer fell sideways in a faint, barely
missing the low-burning candles. The people stared
in fright. After a long spell, the *curandera* rose
slowly and regained her senses. The villagers were
relieved. The torches had almost burned out by this
time.

The *curandera* said, "We must find a way to
control this woman's spirit. I do not know where
she is from. She is angered by her present circumstances. Her spirit turns into a vengeful cat, a
demonic cat of enormous size that kills out of anger
and frustration. We must find someone who has
been to many lands and knows her language. One
of you must go to the coast, to the town of
Acapulco, and find a sailor who can help us understand the demon and her tongue."

That night, two more travelers were killed on
the road by the cactus patch. The danger was still
in the area. The demon cat had killed more
viciously, tearing up the bodies brutally after the
killing.

The villagers waited and waited for their scout
to return from Acapulco. It would take at least a
week for the trip. They prayed and prayed for the
evil to disappear, but the demon's hatred was
growing.

The village scout searched the cantinas in
Acapulco for someone who could help them. After
enduring a few beatings along the way for
bothering an occasional unfriendly drunkard, he

finally found the person for whom he had been searching in a smoke-filled cantina near the docks. It was a grizzle-bearded sea dog, well tempered by the trials of the sea and very knowledgeable in the ways of the Orient. He had been to Japan, been imprisoned in Korea after a shipwreck, and had made many a port on the Chinese mainland. Sipping his *pulque*, the sailor listened to the stories the villager told.

"So, her tormented soul turns into a cat that kills people? The demon must be from Japan, for only there do they tell stories of demon cats. Most of their cats are bobtailed. They believe that a long-tailed cat is evil and has magical powers, and that a cat with four tails is a Cat of Death. The word for four in Japanese, *shi*, also means death," the sailor explained.

"I will go with you and try to help you rid the area of this demonic cat," the sailor finally said.

The villager and the sailor traveled for three and a half days. It was a slow journey because the old sailor was not used to these land trips. It had been a very long time since he had been a land crab, as he enjoyed calling landlubbers. At last they arrived at a small village some distance from the cactus patch, a village that had lost its share of victims to the demon. There, the sailor rested.

The following day, the *curandera* took the sailor to the cactus patch where the strange things were occurring. The sailor stood there on the road and looked at the patch. It was a large area filled with huge cactus trees. Some were flowering; some were filled with prickly pears. He could hear a few birds warbling their lovely songs in the morning sunlight. For the old sailor, this was a beautiful place, something rare after so many years at sea. However, although he sensed no danger, he could smell the stench of death in the air. Even in the daytime this gave him an uneasy feeling.

That night, after talking with the *curandera,* he went to the cactus patch with a large wooden torch and stood across from the patch waiting. He could hear the crickets chirping in the darkness. The air was warm and dry. A slight breeze was blowing.

Suddenly, he felt a cold shiver. As he turned around and raised his torch, a fireball rushed past him above his head. The fireball went across the dirt road and lingered over the patch as if it were studying him. It was flying and moving in slow erratic motions.

"Who are you?" he asked. But the fireball disappeared with a snapping sound. The sailor remembered that in Japan this fireball is called a will-o'-the-wisp. It is the soul of a deceased person as it wanders the earth. Now, in the area where the will-o'-the-wisp had disappeared, stood a giant cat with four tails; its eyes glistened in the light from the sailor's torch. Out of its mouth came hate-filled words.

"For whom are you waiting?" yowled the cat.

"I'm waiting for you!" the sailor shouted back in Japanese. "I have been waiting for you, demon cat."

The cat stood there a long time looking at him. "Who are you?" asked the cat with its four tails nervously swishing.

"I'm a sailor . . . from the sea. Why did you come to this land to spread death and terror?"

"I hate these people! I hate this land! I miss my homeland very much. In my loneliness and terror, after years of waiting to find peace and rest, I have become the monster that I am, killing to take revenge on those who brought me to this desolate place!"

The cat crept closer as it was talking to the old sailor. The man walked with the torch in front of him to prevent the cat from attacking. The cat tried to gain an advantageous position. The old sailor moved backward into the cactus patch.

The cat followed slowly, sometimes yowling in frustration. It wanted to rip this sailor to pieces but was unable to reach him. The cat became furious when the sailor went deep into the patch. It was too big to get around the cactus trunks.

"Mr. Sailor! Mr. Sailor! Come here!" it screamed. The cat knew it could not get to the sailor. It could change itself back into a fireball, but it could not do any harm in that form.

The sailor crouched in the cactus, waiting for the demon cat's next move. It charged at the cactus. It yowled and leaped back in pain when it hit the cactus pads covered with sharp thorns.

It stood there on the road staring at the sailor in the flickering light of his torch. The large cat nervously paced back and forth on the dirt road. It yowled and screeched in frustration. As the morning sun lightened the sky, the growling cat faded to nothing.

The old sailor had a hunch. He started to slowly search the floor of the cactus patch. He moved carefully among the trunks of the cacti searching through the brush, grass, and fallen pads of the cactus plants. He was pricked occasionally by the thorny plants. His torch had long burned out.

As the skies grew brighter, the search was easier. He looked to one side. There it was, a tattered serape faded by time wrapped around a decorated urn. He could make out white and gold cherry blossoms on the exterior of the urn.

He had found the urn at last. He pushed off the worn serape. It fell away easily. He picked up the urn gently with his hands. He did not want to drop and damage it. The sailor carried it out of the cactus patch and went straight to the *curandera's* house. He was tired and sleepy, but he told the healer to go with him to the village of Atoyac where a large cemetery was located.

"We must bury her before nightfall, or else we will be in trouble."

They both left quickly and headed for Atoyac. Once they arrived at Atoyac, they asked the village priest, Padre Juan, to help them bury the Japanese woman's remains in the cemetery. They told him everything that had occurred, and he agreed to help them.

After digging the burial plot at the cemetery, they were joined by other villagers. They wrapped the urn and placed it into a box. They lowered the box into the hole and covered it with earth. The people all prayed for her. The white-haired priest said a short prayer for her, praying for her eternal rest in a place so far from her homeland, Japan.

The next day they placed a tombstone on the grave. The tombstone was inscribed "The Japanese Woman, So Far From Her Homeland Japan/Rest In Peace." From that day on, the demon cat was no longer seen.

As local custom demands, every year on the Day of the Dead the villagers whitewash her stone and cover her grave with marigold flowers. She is not forgotten. Although she was responsible for many deaths, they have long since forgiven her.

As for the old sailor, the day of the burial he returned to put some flowers on the grave and to say goodbye to the Japanese woman. He was thanked by the villagers for helping to eradicate the demon and was rewarded with a small monetary donation. He left for Acapulco, where he disappeared into the world of the cantinas.

If you walk by the cemetery in the village of Atoyac during the evening twilight, you might hear the gentle crying of a woman in the corner of the cemetery. They say it is the Japanese woman crying in her loneliness so far from her beloved homeland.

THE BRUTISH INDIAN

THE BRUTISH INDIAN

The forest path was lush with green plants and occasional flowers. A humming voice could be heard in the humid air. It was the voice of a woodcutter. The tune was an ancient one, passed down by the local Indians. Nobody remembered the words, only the tune. The old woodcutter hummed as he walked along the forest path with a load of tree branches pressing down heavily on his bent back.

"I want a cup of cold water," he suddenly said to himself out loud.

It had been a hard day for him. He was headed back to the village to sell his firewood. He was a simple man, a little awkward in manner and very poor. He came up on the hill and he could see the village in a distant clearing below. There was still a river to cross. The river would be up above his knees. It was getting late, and he would have to cross the river in the darkness.

He stopped to rest and sat down to watch the ants of the forest. They moved in a narrow line, darting and scurrying in one direction or the other. The small creatures fascinated him. In his simple mind, he identified with them. They were always working, with no time to rest.

"Poor small creatures," he thought to himself. "They are probably the souls of evil people who died and are reborn as ants to work until the end of this world. They have their tunnels that go down into the innards of the earth, to the center of Hell where the Devil works them endlessly."

The sun was setting fast. The long shadows of the trees told him that he must hurry or he would be walking the path home in the dark. He trudged steadily along the path with his heavy load of wood. He could hear the crickets starting to chirp here and there in the creeping darkness as he stumbled on the wet rocks of the riverbank. He tried to move carefully among the rocks as he stepped toward the river and into the slow swirling waters.

It was a wide river, and it felt good as the water cooled his tired legs. Suddenly, a long mournful crying sound came drifting across the waters. He stopped to listen for the direction of the sound, but he could only hear the soft swirling of the river past his legs. He stood quietly looking at the silhouette of the tall trees in the forest, but no sound came from there.

An instinct born of centuries of Indian survival told his brain, "Awaken! Something is wrong." But his simple mind only dulled his instinct. He was weary of his heavy load, wishing only to get back to his peaceful home and rest.

Out of the distant darkness came another mournful cry and a long howling scream. He lifted his head quickly and listened. He thought to himself, "It's probably a puma hunting for its evening meal."

He was only halfway across the river when he saw the phantom coming over the water in his direction. It was a huge woman. He marveled at the ghost, this huge apparition moved, floating above the river waters. Her loud mournful screams made the Indian feel sorry for the woman. She looked so lonely and sad. He stood there staring and staring at her approaching form.

He felt no fear of the ghost. His simple mind could not comprehend that he was in mortal danger. He looked at her as if she were an angel from beyond. His dulled senses had not warned him that this ghost was the infamous La Llorona, the crying woman, who roams the rivers at night looking for her children, the little ones she killed by throwing them into a river and drowning them. She was cursed by the gods to find no peace until the end of the world. Whatever foolish mortal met her near the river ran the risk of dying gruesomely.

Here in the middle of the river she found a simple Indian, too humble to comprehend his foolish fate. The woodcutter looked up at the huge ghost. She was towering high above his head like a monster ready to devour its prey. But what fascinated the Indian was the beauty of her face.

"Perhaps she is an ancient Indian princess looking for the portal to the next world. That's why she cries so mournfully."

He stared at the woman towering way above him. She was no longer crying or screaming. Instead, she reached down and grabbed him violently. He felt the pain of her talons sinking deep into his flesh. She lifted him high with a powerful jerk, making his bundle of wood scatter all over the river to be swept away by the current.

The Indian screamed in pain, feeling La
Llorona's sharp talons bite into his flesh as she
lifted him into the air. He could feel the wetness of
his blood oozing from his wounds. Her staring eyes
were malevolent. A slight tremble shook his body,
and he asked her fearfully in a slow drawl, "Why
are you so cruel to me? Why are you hurting me? I
have done nothing to you."

His words had barely cleared his throat when
suddenly she plunged his body into the swirling
waters. He struggled to free himself and to break
loose from her hold, but her grip was too tight and
her talons only sank deeper into his flesh. She lifted him up again. She was like a hungry cat toying
with a mouse, making its victim suffer and cry
before killing it.

Poor dumb woodcutter! He looked again at the
ghostly woman's face. An evil smile was on her lips.
His innermost brain screamed at him that his life
was at stake. Yet the simple woodcutter could only
look into the phantom's eyes deeper and deeper,
trying to understand the brutal treatment he was
enduring. All this time blood and water dripped
from him down into the river, and he was beginning to feel weak.

The Indian screamed out at the ghost, "Why?
Why?" as he stared into the dark, dark pupils of his
tormentor. "Why? Why? Who are you? Where are
you from?" his mind echoed. He could not look
away. Some unknown force kept him staring into
her eyes.

La Llorona felt a piercing sympathy for this
simple Indian. Was he not one of her own kind? An
Indian suffering from centuries of abuse first by
the hated Spaniards and then at the hands of the

mestizos? A primordial feeling stirred in her breast, a bond with this Indian she was tormenting. His cries of pain and his anguished moans washed through her soul.

She had killed many of her own kind before, but this time she knew that she could not do it. She shuddered violently as if something inside was ripping her apart. She dropped the woodcutter into the water as her hands rose and gestured toward the heavens. A long painful and mournful scream came out of her twisted lips. In horrible agony, she lunged upward into the air and swiftly disappeared down the river, still screaming miserable screams mixed with hatred and sorrow.

The Indian fell all the way to the bottom of the river. He quickly fought the current and managed to get on his feet and breathe. He stood there for awhile dripping wet, gasping for air, trying to make sense of what had occurred. As he slowly moved in the direction of the riverbank, he could feel the pain from his wounds.

He would never understand what had happened. He would only remember a moment of terror now etched in his simple mind. He had escaped with his life, the only person who had ever escaped from the death grip of La Llorona. She had taken pity on this poor creature.

The woodcutter still chops his firewood in the forest. He burns copal—an incense—to the ancient Indian gods of his fathers and prays that he never meets the goddess of the rivers again.

If nightfall finds him on the other side of the river, he sleeps in the forest, waiting until daybreak to cross it. When he tells people to stay away from the river after dark, they only laugh at him and say, "Poor dumb woodcutter. He's crazy." Still at night you can hear the cries and screams of La Llorona along the river. Stay away, for you will not escape as the Indian did.

THE WHIRLWIND

THE WHIRLWIND

The boy sat with his dog Mangas outside the small adobe structure that they called home. They sat there in the shade; the boy scratching the dog's head. Mangas had received this name because he was black with white front legs and black paws; it looked like the dog was wearing white sleeves or *mangas.*

The morning was hot and dry, and the boy, whose name was Chicho, didn't want to move around in the heat. He just sat there staring at the distant mountains beyond the fields of corn and past the sandy landscape with its cacti and desert bushes.

"It must be cool on those mountains," he mumbled. He was awakened from his daydreaming by his mother who called to him to come into the house and eat his *pozole,* a soup that deliciously blends hominy and pork.

He yelled back to his mother, "I'm not hungry!"

The heat was very uncomfortable. Chicho didn't feel like moving, but Mangas stood up hungrily wanting to go inside and not miss out on a meal. As the dog started to walk to the house, Chicho grabbed him and pushed him down in the dust. Mangas growled in disappointment and lay there in a bad mood.

Chicho continued his daydreaming. "I wonder what it would be like to fly? To fly like a bird and be free and never have to worry about the heat, just fly to the nearest river and be cool!"

He was surprised when a breeze started blowing, kicking up dust as it drifted by. The cool air hit him ever so lightly in the face, enough to make him feel good. His thoughts were interrupted again by his mother's voice calling out to him.

"Chicho! Go out to the cornfields. Pick some corn for the evening meal. And pick some jalapeño peppers for your father's chili!"

He hated to hear his mother's voice, always wanting something. He did not like to work or to do his chores around the house. He would mutter and walk away angry at having to do what he was told. His muttering on some occasions got him a twisting pinch on the arm or a quick swat on his behind.

His mother would scold him, "Naughty boy, someday you are going to cry for me. I will not be with you all your life!" She would then start to weep and sob, covering her face with her apron.

He would feel ashamed of himself, but his attitude didn't change. At other times he was told, "Don't complain or the demons of the desert will carry you away! Bad boys who don't behave know this!"

Chicho never did anything voluntarily. He always had to be told and reminded to do his chores. He was truly a bad and disobedient boy. He didn't like chopping wood or pumping water for cooking the meals. He really detested any kind of work.

This hot sunny day, while sitting in the shade of

his house, he spotted a whirlwind in the distance. It picked up dust and swirled around and around way up into the sky. It fascinated him. He watched it kick up loose dirt and dry plants, flinging them high into the air.

His mother had warned him not to go near those whirlwinds. They were the handiwork of the demons and devils in the desert. This was their evil dance. Swirling and spinning, they would work themselves up into a sinful passion. Then the whirlwind would dissipate, and the goblins it held would leave to go do their evil deeds in the world.

But knowing Chicho, he would never listen to his elders, much less to his mother. Woe to you young ones who heed not the wisdom of your elders! Woe to you who have no respect for your parents, for they have acquired their wisdom in the pain and suffering of their long years.

Chicho didn't care. He was a young lazy rascal, very unhappy with his life. He wanted to play, eat, sleep, and not worry about the responsibilities of his never-ending chores. He wanted to be like a raven and fly in the sky all day long with no worries in his daily life.

The whirlwind moved in closer and closer, making a soft whistling sound. "What if? . . ." Chicho thought to himself as he got up and started out in the direction of the whirlwind. Mangas bit the boy's trousers and attempted to hold him back, but Chicho was determined to go. He hit Mangas on the jaw, and Mangas let go. Chicho ran toward the whirlwind.

Mangas sensed that his young master was in the process of committing a very foolish act. The dog leaped forward and ran fiercely toward Chicho and the whirlwind. Chicho was by then almost upon the whirlwind.

Suddenly, the wind grabbed Chicho into its swirling mass, while Mangas hearing the boy's screams, jumped in after him, barking and growling, trying to free both himself and Chicho free by biting and scratching at the arms of the demons who were holding them. Boy and dog were fighting for their lives, knowing that unless they got away they would probably end up in some horrible place, probably Hell itself.

The terror that Chicho and Mangas felt made their strength surge so that they fought harder to escape. Soon howls of pain and frustration came from the spinning wind, from the demons who were struggling to keep the two of them. The evil spirits were losing their battle. They were hurting from Mangas' vicious bites.

Finally and unexpectedly, Chicho and Mangas were sent swirling out of the whirlwind. As they skidded to a tumbling stop in the sand, the whirlwind continued speeding onward into the distance, the moans, groans, and screams of the demons who had lost their prey still could be heard.

Chicho patted his dog's head and said, "We're lucky to get away. Who knows what evil was in store for us if the demons had kept us in the whirlwind?"

As he shook the dust from his clothes and began to catch his breath, he suddenly noticed that his hands were dry and crinkled like an old man's. Veins protruded visibly on his hands and his nails were dull. His body was longer and thinner. He was surprised as he looked at himself and saw the body of an old man.

Chicho looked over at Mangas. He was horrified. Beneath the dust, his dog's hair had turned gray and his whiskers white. As Chicho watched his old dog hobble over to him, tears welled in his eyes and ran down his dusty face.

"What happened?" he asked Mangas. But Mangas only looked at him with the eyes of an older dog who couldn't understand itself what had taken place. His master looked so old!

Chicho sat there crying and sobbing. "The whirlwind! The whirlwind! It stole our youth!"

He sat on the ground. Mangas hobbled over and licked his face. Chicho covered his face with his hands and cried in sorrow. The demons of the whirlwind had stolen their youth, Chicho realized. He sobbed and sobbed, and the dog let out a long mournful howl. It was a sad day for both of them.

They finally got up and found the road that would lead back to their home. Chicho didn't understand how they ended up so far from home in the short time that they were in the whirlwind. They walked all day, and at night they slept close together to keep warm in the cold desert. In the early dawn they continued their trip home again.

Chicho cried much of the time, and hunger plagued them both. Some relief came from eating the seedy prickly pear from the numerous cacti in that region. They drank the meaty juice from the succulent fruit.

Finally, they arrived at the area where Chicho remembered his adobe house had once stood. There was only rubble. Broken adobe bricks lay scattered around what remained of the walls of the house. Desert shrubs grew all over. The desert was slowly reclaiming the land. The cornfields were long gone. Everything had been abandoned many years ago.

He stood there in the quiet ruins and called out, *"Mamá! Mamá!"* But only the echoes from the distant hills answered him.

Mangas looked at him with sad eyes. Their home was gone! Gone forever into the quicksand of time. Only a carcass of their former lives remained. The years had passed so swiftly during their time in the whirlwind. Gone was their youth, too. The demons of the whirlwind had lost their prey, but they had exacted their revenge.

Chicho walked over to the edge of a crumbled adobe wall and sat down gently. His old limbs caused him pain when he moved. Mangas slowly came over and lay down beside him. Chicho had tears running down his cheeks. He was an old man with an old dog.

He lived for many more years. Even in his old age, he and his dog Mangas would attempt to chase down a whirlwind whenever one came by. Chicho would hobble after it with his dog at his side to jump into the whirlwind, but they were too slow. Only the demons knew why Chicho and Mangas were chasing whirlwinds. They were trying to enter one to recapture their youth. The swirling demons of the whirlwind would only tease them and laugh at them as the wind swiftly moved away.

The local people called Chicho and Mangas "the crazy old man and his old dog." He was the village idiot who chased whirlwinds. He probably went insane as a punishment for the evil of his youth, people would say. But nobody would ever find out the truth—only Chicho and Mangas knew the story, and even now they can't tell you. They passed on to their fathers and are buried together at the local cemetery.

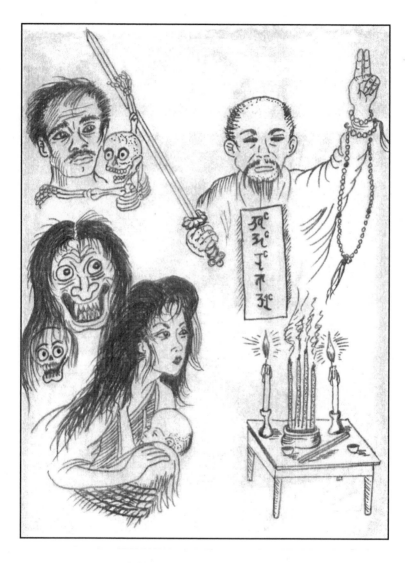

THE CHINESE WOMAN OF THE SEA

THE CHINESE WOMAN
OF THE SEA

On the Pacific side of Baja, California, there is a beach surrounded by rocks. There are many clusters of rocks off the beach in deeper water. Pounding waves hit the rocks and explode into flying foam and water. On the far left side of the beach is a cluster of rocks known to the local people as Seal Rocks. The rocks are used as resting places by seals, sea gulls, and other sea fowl.

Many years ago a coffin washed up on the rocks. The waves kept battering it until it broke into pieces, revealing the body of a young Chinese woman with her baby tied up against her breast with strands of old rope. The waves washed the corpses into a deep crevice in the rocks. The rocky crevice protected the bodies from the violent crashing waves coming in from the sea.

The woman was from a nearby Chinese hamlet. Chinese fishermen and their families had arrived years earlier from upper California in their fishing boats. The coastal current had carried them down, and they had landed in a small cove where they built their houses. With such abundant marine life in the area, they had decided to stay. They made their daily living fishing and diving for the abalone which were plentiful in the cove.

The young woman had drowned only a couple of kilometers away from Seal Rocks Beach. After she drowned, it had taken five days of hard work to recover her body from the deep because of the rough seas. Meanwhile, her baby had refused to eat or drink, and it soon died crying for his mother.

To retrieve her body, the Chinese fishermen had brought a big rock from the beach and tied a rope to a diver. The diver held the rock in his arms and jumped into the sea. Down, down he went into the deep blue water. When he reached the bottom, he could feel tremendous pressure against his small body. He swam over to the corpse, managed to grab her arm, and jerked his line to let the people above know to pull him in. Swiftly and steadily, he was pulled up until he broke the surface of the water gasping for air.

The fishermen had built a coffin, and they tied the woman's baby to her body with old pieces of rope. The mother and child would be together in death as they were in life. They placed the coffin on the fantail of the boat. On their way back to the hamlet, a huge wave arose from the sea and smashed into the boat and washed the coffin into the sea. A riptide carried it away beyond the reach of the small fishing boat. The Chinese fishermen could only wail and cry over their loss. It was hard for them to lose the bodies after the struggle and sacrifice to retrieve the woman's corpse. They could only cry in their misery as the coffin swirled and tossed in the turbulent sea then disappeared from their sight in the ocean waves.

Sometime later, a woman's mournful sobbing and a baby's gentle crying could be heard at Seal Rocks intermingled with the sound of the waves that crashed against the rocks and onto the beach. Only the bravest would venture past the beach at night. Unfortunately, the footpath by the beach was the only way to go to the neighboring villages.

One dark night, an old man—known to people in the villages as *Tigre Acero* or Steel Tiger—was walking along the beach path. He was feeling a little tipsy. He had shared a little *pulque* with his friends at the next village.

"What a beautiful night!" he said to himself.

Just then, he heard a baby crying softly from the distant rocks by the beach. In his drunken mind he thought he was hearing voices. The crying drifted closer and closer. Suddenly, the crying stopped. Everything went quiet, even the crickets were silent. An eerie calm settled over the area. Only the slow steady beat of the old man's sandals on the pathway could be heard. He was aware that something was wrong, but he kept on walking.

He was not scared. He had walked this footpath many times in the past. He was Tigre Acero, the Steel Tiger, the meanest man in the village. But he was much older now. Age had mellowed his temper, yet he still boasted of his fighting youth. The local villagers didn't call him Tiger anymore, only "Old Man Acero."

He continued walking until a soft voice called to him. "Sir! Sir! Help me, please." He was startled by the voice and turned in the direction of the sound. He calmed down quickly. It was a young lady in the shadow of an old tree with low hanging branches. He could see she was holding a bundle in her arms.

"Help me, please!" she said again.

He asked her, "What are you doing here so late at night?"

She replied, "I fell asleep with my baby. We have been walking all day, so I took a nap and just woke up."

He looked at her with curiosity. What was a Chinese woman doing out here by the beach and so late at night? As he mulled over the question, he was interrupted by her. She sadly revealed that she had no place to go.

Acero, being kindhearted in his old age, said to her, "You and your baby can stay with me as long as you wish. I'm a lonely old man, and I need companionship and someone to cook and care for my house. If you agree to these terms, you can stay." Then they continued on their way.

While walking in the darkness, he told her, "You are Chinese, so I won't tell people about you. They will only spread gossip and slander against me. There aren't too many Chinese people around here, except in the fishing hamlet some distance away."

She walked softly behind him, hardly making any noise. He looked back at her. She glowed in the darkness, with the phosphorescent glow of breaking sea waves on a moonlit night. He thought his eyes were playing tricks on him because he was drunk. He kept on walking, looking back every so often to see if she was still with him.

Upon reaching the village, a few dogs started howling. "Strange," he told the Chinese woman, "they usually bark and growl at me. But tonight they stay away and howl."

There was a saying in the village that when a

dog howls at night, somebody has just died. He thought about this and laughed out loud. "Can't be me. I'm still walking around!"

They walked into his home. He showed her the small room that had been his wife's bedroom. She had passed away years before, and he had been forced to live by himself. He missed her very much, but time heals the open wounds of sadness. Now, he was happy again. The Chinese woman would take care of the chores. He would be able to spend more time with his friends in the neighboring village.

He woke up the next morning with an aching head from his hangover. He knew he had too much to drink last night. The woman . . . was that a dream? But the smell of pinto beans and fresh corn tortillas in the stuffy air told him otherwise. He went out to the well, washed himself, and drank a little water. It tasted so good and sweet! He walked back into the house.

All the rooms were dark. The Chinese woman had covered the windows with thick curtains, and very little light came in. When he asked her why, she explained to him that the strong desert sunlight hurt her eyes.

"It's all right. I can live with it," he said.

He thought maybe that's why she was so pale, that the Chinese lived this way. He told her to rest. She then left for her small room.

He called to her, "I'll be going to see my friends in the next village. I'll be back late." She didn't answer him.

As the weeks went by, he started to lose weight. Too much drinking, he thought, and the late hours. Every night when he came down the beach path

after drinking with his friends, the woman would
be waiting for him. Together they walked the path
back to the house. He was usually drunk and
would hum a lively country song, as the girl walked
softly behind him with her baby in her arms.

She always had that strange glow and the smell
of the sea. A fisherman's daughter, Tigre Acero
mused to himself. He asked her what her name
was one night, and she said her name was *Li Ying*,
which means Pear Tree in Chinese. He laughed out
loud when she mentioned her name. He laughed
and laughed.

"You should have a name like María or Luisa or
Rosa," he told her.

She scowled at him. "You are very rude and
have no manners."

He felt bad when she scolded him. He knew
that he had ridiculed her name and had been disrespectful to her. He apologized to her for being so
impolite. She slowly smiled at him, and he knew
she had forgiven him.

He grew even thinner and found it hard to get
around. Even going to visit his friends was becoming difficult. He stayed home more, sitting quietly
with a bottle of tequila on the table. Li Ying would
scurry around the rooms dusting and cleaning. She
would come over to the chair where he was sitting
and stroke his hair and face very gently. He felt
happy with her. But when he looked too long into
her dark almond eyes, he was afraid.

Since he was not feeling well these days and
was no longer able to visit his friends, they began
to visit him instead. They came in the daytime
because it was easier for them to walk the beach
path and they were afraid of the beach at night.

They would always come over with a couple of bottles of tequila. They would open the curtains wide and let the sunlight in.

"You shouldn't live in the dark," they told him, "That's why you are becoming so pale. Pretty soon you'll look like a gringo!"

Whenever his friends came over, Li Ying and her baby disappeared. He did not find this too strange, thinking perhaps she was bashful and fearful of his rustic friends. She would always come back at night. The dogs would howl when she arrived. She told Tigre Acero it was because they smelled a stranger; she was not of Mexican-Indian stock like the rest of the people.

His health continued to get worse. He remained in bed more and more. She had to help him get up. He hobbled around with a stick as a cane. His skin was getting paler and ghostly. His eyes were beginning to protrude from his sunken face. His friends would drop by more often, and Li Ying would disappear with her baby more often. He never told anyone about her, not even his friends.

He used to go to the market to buy his food. Now a local woman from the market had to deliver his foodstuffs. She did not like to remain in the house. Something frightened her. She did not understand what it was, but she didn't discuss it with him. When people came to the house, they could also sense something strange. But they couldn't see Li Ying, so no one knew of her presence in Acero's house. Only the dogs knew. Only Tigre Acero could see her. He was a bewitched man.

He had grown fond of Li Ying and even loved her, though he would never admit it. With the passing of days and months, he knew he needed her more. He looked forward to seeing her return in the evening, especially now that his health was failing.

One morning, a very good friend of his named Cruz came by to see him. He had heard that Old Man Acero was very sick and probably would not last another month. Maybe it was tuberculosis.

"I'm going to bring the healer, to see you," Cruz said. "She should have come hee a long time ago; then you wouldn't be so sick."

After Cruz left, Acero could hear Li Ying softly singing a Chinese song to her baby. The tune sounded very peculiar to his ears, and it caused him to shake from some unknown fear. He had never heard her sing before. To him, it sounded like a funeral chant.

Finally, his friend Cruz arrived with Amalia, the *curandera* or healer. Amalia was a short heavy woman with sharp Indian features. As soon as she walked into the room, she stopped and stood still for a long time.

"Something is very wrong! I sense a powerful evil presence here," she said, "I can't do much for your friend." Her words stopped cold. She trembled and ran out of the door of the house, a look of horror was on her face. She looked back as if a demon were chasing her. She kept on running. For an old fat woman she moved fast, as if in fear for her life.

Cruz was surprised by her actions. "She's a fraud! Nothing but a fraud! And she calls herself a healer!" Acero looked at him with disappointment.

"Don't worry, my friend," Cruz said, "I have another idea. I'll be back later. Don't worry. I'll be back!"

Li Ying came out of her room and sat beside the old man in bed.

"Where have you been?" he asked her.

"I was in my room," she said, "with my baby." She looked at him with a twisted smile on her lips. Her black almond eyes were gazing at him fiercely. He had never seen that look before. He felt so helpless and scared.

Later that afternoon, his friend Cruz arrived. "I'm sorry I'm late," he said, "but I had to go by boat to a village and pick up a healer who knows herbs and medications. His name is Mr. Tong. He is from the Chinese fishing village down the coast."

As soon as Mr. Tong walked in, a strange thing happened to Old Man Acero. He started to shake and tremble and began to cry.

"Why do you look so startled, Mr. Acero? Why are you shaking so much? Why do you fear me?" Mr. Tong placed his hand on Acero's chest and Acero fainted. Mr. Tong looked around slowly, like a cat sensing a mouse. He could feel the evil in the house, but he was not afraid.

The Buddhist talisman he wore on his chest would protect him. It was a yellow strip of paper with Sanskrit characters written on it in red ink. Mr. Tong was not only a healer, but also an exorcist. He was a very respected man in the community, a scholar of the ancient schools that have long since disappeared on the Chinese mainland.

"Who lives here with you?" Mr. Tong asked the old man when he recovered from his faint.

Acero hesitated, then said in a weak voice, "A young Chinese woman and her baby." Tears were coming from his eyes.

"Where did she come from, and what is her

name?"

"She said her name was Li Ying. I met her about a year ago on the beach at Seal Rocks one night coming home." Acero told Mr. Tong the whole story of their meeting.

Mr. Tong looked at Mr. Acero and said, "You are in great mortal danger! I do not have time to explain. Mr. Cruz will remain here with you tonight."

Mr. Tong pulled out yellow sheets of paper from his bag, a bottle of red ink, and a brush. He started to write Sanskrit characters on the papers. He then pasted these sheets of paper on the doorways and windows with glue he had hastily made from rice flour.

"She cannot return as long as the placards remain where they are," he explained to Cruz. "There is an ancient Chinese belief that there are two spirits, or souls, inside a human. There is a higher spirit and a lower spirit. When a person dies, the higher spirit leaves the body and the lower spirit remains until the body begins to decompose. Then the lower spirit leaves the body and returns back to its origin to be reborn again with the higher spirit."

"Sometimes, for reasons unknown, the lower spirit remains in the body and does not want to depart this earth. The lower spirit becomes an evil vampire that will prey on humans, slowly draining their life force and killing them. This is what is happening to your friend," said Mr. Tong.

"The Chinese woman fits the description of Li Ying, who drowned about ten years ago. Her body and that of her baby were lost in stormy seas. Look after your friend, Mr. Cruz. I will go to Seal Rocks.

Li Ying's ghost can not harm me. The Lord Buddha
will help me put her miserable spirit to rest." That
ended the conversation as he walked away with his
lantern glowing and swinging in the darkness of
the night.

Meanwhile, Li Ying had returned to the house.
She was surprised to find that she could not get
close to the entrance because it was covered with
the holy placards that Mr. Tong had glued to the
doors and windows. They blocked her path.

She cried out to Acero, "Please! Please! Let me
come in!" Cruz was frightened and remembered
what Mr. Tong had said about her being a vampire.
Li Ying's baby started to wail.

"Please, if you love me, remove those papers
from the door and let me in." Acero made a desperate effort to get up, but Cruz held him down. Acero
could not stand to hear her sad, mournful pleas.

Then there was quiet. Only the howling of the
village dogs could be heard. She had disappeared
as Acero lay in bed crying and Cruz watched over
him.

As Tong moved closer to the beach, Li Ying
appeared with her baby in the shadow of a tree. He
said to her, "I have come to release you from this
earth. You should never have remained. So tell me,
where is your body?"

"I will not tell you!" she screamed at him, bar-
ing her huge fangs, "I will destroy you first. I will
not leave this earth!" She made a move as if to
lunge at him. But she suddenly noticed his talisman and backed away swiftly.

"You must go," he told her, "In your present
state you are a demon doing evil. This must come
to an end! I will remain here until dawn. I think I

know where your bones are!" He pulled out a string of Buddhist prayer beads and commenced to pray the sutras.

She screamed at him and pleaded, "I don't want to go. Have mercy on me and my baby! Please! Please! You must let me exist. I must exist! I will stop you!"

"No," he said, "You must leave this earth and go on to your next fate, to be reborn again in the cosmos." He would no longer listen to her and continued to pray in a low voice.

Li Ying cried all night, cradling her baby. In the early dawn, she faded away into the air, still crying very sadly in heart-rendering sobs. She knew that she had lost the battle.

As soon as she had disappeared, Mr. Tong stopped praying and started to walk down the beach toward Seal Rocks. He walked over to the rocks in the low morning tide, climbed up on them, and started to search.

He went over to a large crevice in the rocks. There he found the remains of Li Ying and her baby, their skeletons bleached by the sun, broken up a little, but still intact. The crevice had protected the bones from being scattered by breaking waves. Mr. Tong worked his way down into the crevice and stood there saying a Buddhist prayer for the dead. Then gently, one by one, he placed the bones in a small bag that he had brought with him. He gathered all the bones, then he headed back to Acero's house. It had been a long night for him and he was tired, but the job was not done yet.

He stopped to talk with the Cruz family and with Acero. After refreshing himself with food and drink, he bid them farewell. Old Man Acero would survive to live many more years. He would miss Li Ying, even after he found out that she was draining him of life.

Mr. Tong returned back to his village, and everybody was happy that he had found the remains of Li Ying and her baby. He never mentioned to anyone how he had managed to find their bones or under what circumstances. That was a secret he would take to his grave. A funeral was held for the remains, then they were cremated. Mr. Tong had insisted upon the cremation. He knew that this was the only way to force the lower spirits to leave the bodies and go back to the cosmos.

The people in the village talked about Mr. Acero's miraculous recovery, but they never learned what had really taken place. But even if they had known, they would not have believed it. The villagers said he walked around muttering to himself. Maybe his excessive drinking messed up his brain, they would say. But only he knew the secret of the Chinese Woman of the Sea.

LA LLORONA OF THE MOON

LA LLORONA OF THE MOON

It was a quiet night with a full moon gliding across a glittering star-studded sky. A warm wind was blowing. Michela was awake, sitting up on her bed and looking at the stars. They seemed to her like shiny gems suspended from strings in the sky. She did not feel like sleeping because of an argument she had had with her mother about cleaning the ashes out of their woodburning adobe oven.

"Bad girls are punished for being disrespectful to their parents and their elders," said her mother.

Michela laughed. "I don't care, and I don't believe in your Indian gods. They're only idols that don't move or speak. I'm not afraid of old foolishness."

Her mother looked at her in alarm, tears in her eyes. She told her daughter, "The gods of your ancestors will never forgive you for desecrating their images with vile words!"

Michela ran out of the house, climbed a huge pile of rocks, and sat in the shade of the largest boulder where she grabbed a stick and tormented a lizard lying in a crevice away from the hot desert sun. She sat there alone, looking back at the house, wishing she could escape her hard life in the desert.

Her father had left for the United States to earn a few more *pesos*, but he never returned home again. She had asked her mother about her father.

"Why doesn't he come back?"

Her mother always told her, "He will return one of these days."

After a few months she quit asking and gave up on him. She had a feeling that she would probably never see him again, that he was gone forever.

The evening with its red-orange colored sky approached fast. Michela, who had fallen asleep on top of the cold rock, awoke startled. It was time to go back to the house and eat. She jumped off the rock and started walking toward the house, kicking up sand with her bare feet. She saw her mother cooking by the kitchen window. The strong smell of pinto beans and corn tortillas made her tummy growl from hunger.

Nothing was said when Michela sat down on the mat to eat with her mother. She was ashamed of the things she had said earlier that day. She felt the steady gaze of the Indian idols from their niche on the far wall. Her mother had lit a candle at their feet. The flickering light made the idols look like they were moving and pointing at her. She felt a shiver of fear run down her spine.

After eating their meager meal, her mother went to the doorway and waited for Uncle Edmundo to arrive. He came once a week on horseback, leading a burro loaded with sacks of beans and corn. That was the only way Michela and her mother survived in the desert.

Edmundo tried to get his sister to move in with him and his wife, but she refused, saying her hus-

band might return some day and that when that
happened, he would not find them home.

"That accursed man is not going to return," her
brother told her.

"Don't talk bad of my husband, little brother,"
she cautioned him softly.

That evening, after putting the sacks on the
kitchen floor, Edmundo got ready to leave.

"Be careful going home!" his sister told him.
"It's a full moon. It's the night of the La Llorona of
the Moon!"

It was a local superstition that on the first
night of the full moon the Wailing Woman was
allowed to escape her bonds from the rivers and go
gather all the evil souls that she could find—like
thieves, murderers, bad children, and other types
of horrible people. She carried her harvest down
deep into the inner core of the earth where eternal
fires burned and the unfortunate were placed in
flaming pits to await their gruesome fate. There
the ancient Indian gods, angered because they had
been forgotten, would sacrifice the foolish mortals
as in the days of old. Thus, the gods would be satis-
fied and the sun would continue to rise over the
land.

Michela thought of her mother's words, "Bad
girls are punished!" Those words made her uneasy
as she sat in a dark corner of the room. Her tired
mother was sleeping soundly in the other room.
She could hear her labored breathing.

Then Michela saw it! In the eerie triangle that
the moonlight cast on the adobe-block floor, a mist
was forming. A tall thin woman materialized,
pointing her finger at Michela. Michela was frozen

with fright, unable to scream. Tears welled in her eyes.

"You, young child, are a very bad girl!" whispered La Llorona. "You have caused the ancient Indian gods of your ancestors to demand an end to your vile ways. You have no respect for your mother or your elders. You do not respect the gods who gave you life. Therefore, it is their decree that this night you are cursed to go with me and forfeit the life given to you. Step into the moonlight where I can see you. I cannot see you in the shadows!"

Michela could hardly speak, but in a small squeaky voice she screeched, "NO! I don't want to go with you!"

The face of the Llorona became twisted with rage, "I'll take you with me!" she said. But as she reached to grab Michela, her bony clawed hands dissolved in the darkness. La Llorona of the Moon had no power in the shadows, only in the moonlight.

La Llorona moved as close as she could within the moonlight, very close to the trembling Michela. "You better give me your hand, girl. I only have to wait for the moonlight to reach your corner and then you will be mine. So why are you being a bad girl? Come give me your hand," La Llorona said, her sharp teeth sparkling in the moonlight.

Michela flattened herself against the wall. She could not scream to her mother. She had lost her voice. She hoped that the moonlight that now was inching toward her feet would not touch any part of her body.

La Llorona of the Moon moved closer and closer as the moon, moving across the sky slowly, ate up the safety of the shadows. The woman's beady eyes reminded Michela of a deadly rattlesnake's before it struck and bit the desert mice. The mice, after they had been bitten, shook and died slowly when the poison did its job. She, too, felt strong fear as her time on earth slipped away. The moonlight was almost touching her toes, only a few centimeters left.

Suddenly, it started receding away. The moonlight had reached the far angle of the window and was moving away from Michela. The moon didn't care who won or lost the battle for life.

La Llorona growled. Her prey, whom she had had so close to her talons, was now escaping. It filled her with rage. Michela was escaping in the growing shadows. La Llorona looked at Michela and said in an enraged voice, "You! You will not escape me. You have won tonight, but I will come back again and again." Hatred filled the Llorona's face. "I will return. You will not escape from me!" were her last words as she slowly faded into a thin mist and disappeared.

Michela sat down slowly on her bed. Her eyes were flowing freely with tears. She was still trembling from the horror-filled moments.

"And you ask, my child, what happened to Michela? Who knows? As for her fate, who can read the future? What will be, will be!" the storyteller exclaims.

THE OWL

THE OWL

It arrived every night and landed in the branches of the cottonwood beside the old weather-
beaten house. Late at night it would start to hoot and
break the silence of the darkness. The owl would
hoot until the early morning hours. It was said in the
barrio that if a man held a grudge against another
person, he could—with the proper secret incanta-
tions—change himself into an owl and fly out at
night, or even during the day, and bewitch his hated
adversary. He could sit on a fence or in a tree and
hoot to torment his victim to death.

The woman who lived in the house was startled
by the sound. Fear came to her face. Her hands
trembled. "Why? Why?" she said out loud to her
husband and her four sons, who stared at her with
puzzled eyes and fear. Her husband told her to
calm down and pay no heed to the old superstition
that the owl was a human in bird form. She would
not listen to him.

Her husband tried every night to calm her
fears, but with the passing of days she became
more frightened. It was becoming a problem for the
whole family. Perhaps it was a man who held a
grudge or wished evil upon her, and in the night

came to torment her with his evil hooting. Something had to be done.

So that night her sons waited for the owl with a small bore rifle in the shadows of a cactus patch. There was a quarter-moon in the sky, and bright glistening stars pulsed overhead. Suddenly, they heard the owl land in the branches of the cottonwood tree with a fast swishing sound. They all looked up toward the upper branches, slowly scanning them. Then one of the boys spotted the small silhouette of the owl on one of the branches. He tugged at his older brother's sleeve and quickly pointed to the small shadow in the tree. They saw it!

The elder brother pointed his rifle very slowly and took aim carefully . . . BAM! He fired once. The bullet ripped the leaves and bark off the tree. A branch shuddered violently. The owl darted out of the tree and flew towards the distant forest across the field from the house.

He had missed! All of them felt disappointed. They had failed to avenge their mother. The evil owl had won the battle.

Their mother, still frightened, occasionally broke down and cried. Their father's irritability was showing in his short temper. Despite their determination, the brothers had failed to destroy the owl and discover who their mother's tormentor was. But their mother forgave their failed attempt and indicated that, at least for the time being, they could sleep in peace. But she feared the owl would return again.

On the following night, the brothers took their post by the cactus patch and waited. The youngest one looked up toward the upper branches of the prickly pear cactus and saw a fruit on the highest

of them. It looked so much like an owl just sitting
there staring at him in the darkness. He looked
away a little frightened. For awhile he thought he
saw the pear move. His brothers kept staring up at
the branches of the cottonwood tree, but nothing
came that night.

The following night the brothers waited again,
and their patience paid off. A small dark object
came fluttering in, sending a few dry leaves down
as it settled on a branch in the tree. The oldest
brother spotted the owl and slowly raised his rifle.
Its long cold black barrel lifted up in a slow steady
motion. A shattering sound came from the rifle as
it discharged its deadly slug toward its target. The
rustle of leaves could be heard as a small lifeless
bundle tumbled and dropped down onto the earth.
They had killed the beast. Never again would it
bother anyone.

They picked the bird up by one of its claws,
walked into a field away from the house, and threw
it down on the ground on a patch of dry grass. They
all looked down at the poor lifeless creature. Could
this be an evil man? They would leave it lying
there and would come back in the morning when
the sun's rays would transform this creature back
into its human form. Then they would know who
the evil person was who had been tormenting their
mother.

They walked back to the house and informed
their parents of their deed. Their father only
shrugged his shoulders, but their mother was joy-
ous. At last she was free from her tormentor and
the owl's curse!

In the early morning, the youngest brother ran
toward the field in eager anticipation to see the

transformation that should by now have taken place in the rays of the morning sun. He arrived at the spot breathing heavily and glanced down at the stiff bird.

It lay very still like the dead red-winged black-birds he had often seen in the marshes. He waited to see the owl change in the sunlight, but nothing happened. It only lay there cold and lifeless with its large eyes open in death.

Poor bird, poor bird, he thought, as tears formed in his eyes. He would never again believe in the curse of owls, devils, or spirits. They were only stories. Owls were only birds, not humans.

Down through the centuries had come the tales and superstitions of our Mexican Indian ancestors. Here in the glowing sunlight, a young boy's beliefs were dying, fleeing forever back through the portal of times past. No one would be left to pass on the tales of spirits who had once roamed unleashed in the world.

Death came not only to the owl, but to the ancient traditions of the elders who had lost the battle against the new gods of science and technology. Still, sometimes if you stop to listen, you might hear the soft murmurs and whisperings of the people of old slowly drifting by in the wind.